"Now promise not _____ *_____,"* Fate said.

"I'm getting a crick in my back from this Rudolph Valentino number you're doing," C.J. evaded.

"Promise."

C.J. wished suddenly that she had long fingernails so that she could dig them into his chest. "I never make promises I can't keep."

"Then promise you'll *try* not to get mad at me."

"And deprive myself of my only pleasure? No way. Will you please let me go before I'm convinced you're more depraved than I originally thought you were?"

Fate sighed and allowed her to straighten, dropping his arm when she was in balance again. "As I believe I've remarked once before, you're a cruel lady. I don't ask for much, after all—"

"Of course not," she interrupted ironically, giving the crushed flowers in her arms a disgusted look. "Just look what you've done! They're ruined."

"Sorry about that." He didn't sound it.

"I'll bet. You're a menace, Maestro, an absolute menace."

"I aim to please," he disclaimed modestly.

"Can't you be serious just for a minute?"

"Oh, but I am." He smiled slowly. "I've been serious all along, pixie. You just haven't realized it yet."

WHAT ARE *LOVESWEPT* ROMANCES?

They are stories of true romance and touching emotion. We believe those two very important ingredients are constants in our highly sensual and very believable stories in the *LOVESWEPT* line. Our goal is to give you, the reader, stories of consistently high quality that may sometimes make you laugh, sometimes make you cry, but are always fresh and creative and contain many delightful surprises within their pages.

Most romance fans read an enormous number of books. Those they truly love, they keep. Others may be traded with friends and soon forgotten. We hope that each *LOVESWEPT* romance will be a treasure—a "keeper." We will always try to publish

LOVE STORIES YOU'LL NEVER FORGET
BY AUTHORS YOU'LL ALWAYS REMEMBER

The Editors

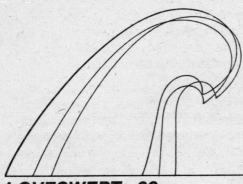

LOVESWEPT • 32

Kay Hooper

C.J.'S Fate

BANTAM BOOKS • TORONTO • NEW YORK • LONDON • SYDNEY

C. J.'S FATE

A Bantam Book / February 1984

LOVESWEPT and the wave device are trademarks of
Bantam Books, Inc.

All rights reserved.
Copyright © 1984 by Kay Hooper.
Cover art copyright © 1984 by Max Ginsburg.
This book may not be reproduced in whole or in part, by
mimeograph or any other means, without permission.
For information address: Bantam Books, Inc.

ISBN 0-553-21638-4

Published simultaneously in the United States and Canada

Bantam Books are published by Bantam Books, Inc. Its
trademark, consisting of the words "Bantam Books" and the
portrayal of a rooster, is Registered in U.S. Patent and Trade-
mark Office and in other countries. Marca Registrada. Bantam
Books, Inc., 666 Fifth Avenue, New York, New York 10103.

PRINTED IN THE UNITED STATES OF AMERICA

O   0 9 8 7 6 5 4 3 2 1

*For Pam
and the conference in Atlanta
where this book was conceived.*

One

"C.J., can't you put that book down for ten minutes?"

The exasperated voice, coming from the willowy blonde seated next to C.J. in the cab, contained more than a thread of real irritation. C.J. lifted her burnished copper head and directed a somewhat quizzical look at her friend, then sighed and marked her place, closing the heavy book and leaving it to rest on her lap. "Sorry, Jan," she murmured.

Jan leaned forward to address the third occupant of the cab, who was sitting on the other side of C.J. "Want to bet she starts reading again the moment we check in?"

The brunette on C.J.'s right shook her head with a long-suffering sigh, her brown eyes merry. "That's the trouble with geniuses—they just can't stop *being* geniuses."

"I'm not a genius, Tami," C.J. protested, her quiet voice mild but very slightly impatient.

"Lord knows that just looking at you no one

1

would take you for a brain," Jan said. "You're no bigger than a pixie, and those ridiculous yellow eyes make you look like a bewildered kitten!"

"It's disgusting!" Tami chimed in, her voice lifting in mock outrage. "All the men cluster around you like bees at a honey pot, until you utterly dumbfound them by saying very seriously that Charlemagne was a terrific king—or whatever he was—and that the Romans were great people in spite of the orgies."

C.J. sighed again as her friends' laughter attacked her ears from both sides. They meant well—they really did. But since she had spent both school days and vacations with them all through the years, these kinds of comments were beginning to grow stale.

If asked, C.J. would have replied quite honestly that the tradition of marriage seemed a fine idea and was, after all, what one made of it. To each his own.

Her "own" was blessed singleness. The love of her life was history; no flesh-and-blood man had succeeded in peeling away so much as one layer of that set of abstractions she had long ago wrapped herself in. C.J. saw nothing wrong with that, nothing missing from her life. She was well-traveled, very well educated, and perfectly capable of holding her own in any social situation. The problem was—said her friends—that she didn't particularly care one way or the other about the *normal* feminine preoccupations.

Her copper hair was curly and kept short for convenience; it rarely saw a brush and never a beauty salon. She wore whatever she happened to pull from closet or drawer, usually casual slacks or jeans and, depending on the season, a sweater or T-shirt. She made no effort to cover with makeup the light sprinkling of freckles on her nose, or to emphasize the catlike slant or color of her tawny eyes. And far from encouraging the attentions of a man, she was more likely to fix him with a ruthlessly clear-seeing gaze, and demand to know what all the pretty speeches were for.

Still, her friends had tried. During the last ten years, they had "fixed her up" with one man after another. She had been ruthlessly pulled from the books in her study time after time to attend a party, see a play, hear a concert. And vacations had been riddled with seemingly casual meetings with suitable, hopefully interesting bachelors. C.J. had only the vaguest recollection of faces and none at all of names.

Four of her friends were now married and Kathy, the last to succumb to the lure of "happily ever after," was scheduled to trip down the aisle exactly one week from today.

The result, unfortunately for C.J., was that her friends were now more determined than ever to see her meet her own Prince Charming. She was aware they would give her no peace until she demonstrated herself to be a perfectly normal female and got married. Or had an affair. Even a fling would give them hope.

Jolted from her thoughts when the cab lurched on an icy spot in the road, she glanced past Jan and out the window at the snow-covered landscape. "Why," she complained mildly to the other two, "did we have to come West to find snow? Boston was blanketed with it when we left. And why does Kathy absolutely *have* to get married in a ski lodge? She met Patrick on a hockey field." She was referring to one of the three girls in the cab behind them.

The other two appeared to have no difficulty understanding her. Jan shrugged. "Kathy's parents were married in Aspen, so she figures it'll be a good omen. The only thing she remembers about them is that they were very much in love."

C.J. sighed. "Well, anyway, I don't see why I couldn't have flown out next weekend. The guys are."

"Only because they can't get away until then," Jan pointed out calmly. "Besides, I think we should try to get the guys out here sooner; the weathermen are predicting a blizzard for next Friday."

Sneaking a glance at Jan's face, C.J. said experimentally, "I'll have time to study—"

As she'd expected, Jan cut her off and immediately began talking about all the fun they were sure to have at the lodge, all the handsome men who were sure to dot the slopes—like ducks in a shooting gallery, C.J. thought wryly.

Listening only vaguely to the song she had heard too many times before, C.J. looked down at the book in her lap and thought wistfully of her cozy apartment and the study room of the library. She'd never be able to get any research done; the girls would see to that. They'd have her busy from morning to night.

Protesting the plans of her friends would do no good at all. Oh, she could have stopped the matchmaking with a few well-chosen words. Cold, cruel words. But she could no more have done that than she could walk on water; it wasn't in her nature to hurt anyone deliberately.

And they were her friends. They thought they knew what was best for her.

From the time they'd met as little girls in first grade, they had been friends. Twenty years lay between then and now, years of sharing little-girl things, and teenage things, and adult things. Experiences. Thoughts. Problems.

They had composed a sort of magic circle, closing ranks protectively when problems arose, and opening a place for someone that one of their number cared for. First boyfriends, and then husbands.

Staring blindly down at the book in her lap, C.J. thought of the past twenty years, and knew she could never tell her friends that she didn't want or need their help now. If it made them happy to try and find a husband for her, then so be it.

But she was nonetheless conscious of an odd restlessness within her. If there were only some way of reassuring them kindly. If there were only some way . . .

The lodge was a vast and modern building, square and without any of the Alpine features popular in the ski areas of Colorado. With the holidays just past, it wasn't crammed to capacity, but it did boast a respectable number of winter-sports fans.

And those fans were very much in evidence as the cabs drew up in front of the lodge. Laughing groups of men and women were shouldering skis and heading in various directions as they tramped happily from the building, making their ways to beginner slopes or to the lifts and the more advanced slopes high above them.

C.J. stood by the cab and watched the comings and goings, only absently listening to the closer confusion of her friends sorting luggage and chattering among themselves.

Nearly an hour later, she was standing in the opened door of her room and nodding patiently as Jan scolded her for the third time.

"I mean it, C.J.—no studying! You need a break,

even if you won't admit it. We barely got you to come up for air during Christmas, and you were going flat out for months before that. Promise!"

"I already promised, Jan," C.J. reminded wearily.

"Sure." Jan didn't sound convinced. "Well, we're going to call the guys and let them know we made it. Dinner's not served for another hour or so, but we'll meet here in about thirty minutes so we can go down and check the place out. How's that?"

"Fine." C.J. couldn't help but smile as her friend's blue eyes swept her sweater and jeans with an all-too-familiar expression of exasperation.

"And could you please change into something a little more presentable? You look like an urchin, damnit!" Jan sighed and her eyes softened unexpectedly. "Sweetie, can't you make an effort just this once? It won't hurt and, knowing you, you'd even enjoy yourself."

C.J. looked at her curiously. "What do you mean by that?"

Jan smiled a little ruefully. "You enjoy the unexpected, C.J. Your problem is that you conquer things too quickly. I think you get bored."

"What's your point, Jan?" C.J. asked uncertainly.

"My point, my dear, is that you can never learn all there is to know about a man."

So . . . they were back to the matchmaking again. But Jan's remark interested C.J. for some reason. "Oh?" she prompted.

"Definitely. Every day brings a surprise. Try it—you might just find the opposite sex fascinating." With an odd little smile, Jan moved on down the hall to her own room.

C.J. closed her door and leaned against it thoughtfully for a moment. Then she dismissed her friend's advice impatiently. Jan was just up to her old tricks, that was all.

Unpacking automatically, C.J. put her things

away with her usual neatness. And then, mindful of Jan's plea, she changed clothes. The slacks and bulky sweater were not, seductively speaking, much of an improvement over the jeans and sweater from before, but they were slightly more presentable. Truth to tell, C.J. didn't own a single article of clothing which could have been termed even remotely sexy.

She paused in front of the mirror to run her fingers casually through her short curly hair and then remained for a few moments, staring at her reflection. She turned sideways and drew the sweater tightly beneath her breasts. Without conceit, she knew that her figure was very good—and somewhat startling for so petite a woman. And her legs, according to the girls' envious remarks, were "the most spectacular pair in the group."

With a sigh, C.J. allowed the sweater to assume its normal bulky shape and turned away from the mirror. What was wrong with her, for heaven's sake? Why this growing restlessness, this odd feeling of dissatisfaction with herself? Had Jan been right? *Did* she become bored with something once the challenge and excitement were gone?

Not history, of course. It still was, and always had been, new and exciting. But something else? Was she bored with herself? She had watched her friends grow and change for twenty years; hadn't she changed as well? Or was she still the same slightly scruffy schoolgirl, a bit cynical and yet drawn to the adventure, the challenge, of learning?

C.J. shook her head irritably and headed for the door. Nonsense. It was just Jan putting stupid ideas into her head, and causing her to question herself for the first time in years.

She went out into the hall, leaned back against the door, and folded her arms. Resolutely she fixed her eyes on the wall across from her and turned her mind to the thesis she was working on.

"C.J., would you like to borrow my lipstick?" It was Ann, her blond curls in their normal enormously attractive disarray, violet eyes gently questioning.

C.J. blinked, automatically taking in Ann's beautifully matched sweater-and-slack set. "No, thanks," she muttered and added with certain self-knowledge, "I'd only chew it off in ten minutes."

Jan emerged from her room at that moment, and came toward them. Her first words were to C.J. "Do you call that an improvement?"

"There's nothing like a friend for a kick in the ego," C.J. murmured, as though to herself.

"You ask for it. Constantly." Jan was unrepentant.

"I did the best I could, Jan."

"Sure. And I'm the queen."

"How do you do?"

Jan sighed. "I haven't been able to get a rise out of you in twenty years. Do you have any idea how frustrating that is?"

"I can imagine."

Susan was next to enter the fray. Tall, naturally regal, every red hair of her striking head in place, she strolled down the hall toward them. Cool green eyes swept C.J. in an automatic appraisal. "Only your sense of color saves you from total disaster," she said calmly.

"Thank you," C.J. said meekly.

"It wasn't a compliment."

Kathy and Tami joined them a moment later. Tami merely groaned in exasperation when she looked at C.J., but Kathy was more voluble.

"You shouldn't have gotten all dressed up just

for us." She tucked a strand of long auburn hair behind one ear and sent a brown-eyed glare at C.J.

Meditatively, C.J. said, "I think I'll put an ad in the paper when we get back to Boston. 'Five friends for sale, rent, loan, or take over payments. Cheap.' "

Ignoring this defensive shot, Jan announced to the others, "Girls, we have to do something about C.J." She gestured for the others to huddle across the hall from their victim. Kathy broke from the strategy session a moment later, exclaiming that she'd forgotten her sweater and dashing down the hall to her room. The others continued to plan.

Accustomed to these tactics—and not the slightest bit offended by them—C.J. watched rather wearily. Around and around in her mind raced her earlier, incompleted wish. *If only* . . .

She fished her key from her pocket and unlocked her door with some vague idea of going back inside and putting on lipstick or something to appease her friends. Holding the door slightly open, she paused to stare down the hallway toward the elevators. That was when she saw the man, and a wave of uncharacteristic recklessness surged through her. Along with a wild idea.

Well, why not? There was enough romance jammed into her history-inclined mind to fake a romance. Wasn't there? A mysterious stranger and secret meetings . . . star-crossed lovers, perhaps? And at least it would get her friends off her back!

The man was tall, casually dressed in sweater and slacks, and moved with easy, loose-limbed grace.

When he was abreast of the crowd, his eyes flicked over her friends and then met C.J.'s intent gaze. He smiled, and that was all C.J. needed.

Still holding the door partly open, C.J. took a

step forward, caught the startled stranger's hand and drew him quickly toward her. Looking up at him with an unintentionally bewitching smile, she said in a low, breathy voice just loud enough for her friends to hear, "Darling, I'm so glad you could make it after all!" Before the girls could see his bemused expression, she pulled him swiftly into the room.

She left the door open a crack, then said sweetly to her stunned friends, "Excuse us . . . please." And gently shut the door.

Unaware that she was still holding the stranger's hand, C.J. put her ear to the door to listen to the numb silence outside.

"Uh . . . pardon me—" the stranger began in a deep voice.

"Ssshh!" C.J. warned absently, her lips curving into a delighted smile as the silence outside broke into a babble of disbelief.

"Was that *C.J.*?"

"Why didn't she tell us, damnit?"

"*Who* is that gorgeous man?"

"I didn't think C.J. even *knew* how to look at a man that way—"

"What's going on? Where's C.J.?" It was Kathy, apparently newly emerged from her room.

"I need a drink," Jan said firmly.

"I need *two*," Tami chimed in, her voice dazed.

"But *what's going on*?" Kathy's wail faded as she followed the others down the wide corridor to the elevators.

Grinning in delight, C.J. turned away from the door. That was when she realized that she was holding a strong male hand. Swiftly, she released it. Her eyes traveled hesitantly up to the stranger's face, and widened slightly. Her grin died a startled death.

He was handsome by anybody's standards. He

looked, she thought vaguely, rather like an Indian. Raven's-wing black hair, unreadable dark eyes set beneath slanted brows, high cheekbones, lean jaw, and the most sensuous mouth she had ever seen. And he was regarding her with a speculation she found extremely disconcerting.

"I—I suppose you want an explanation?" she ventured, the note of hope in her voice telling him clearly that she wished he'd just leave.

"Oh, I think I already have one," he said coolly, and without another word pulled her firmly into his arms.

Astonished both at the suddenness of his action and at the unfamiliar sensation of being crushed against a masculine chest, C.J. fought to organize her vocal cords into productive speech.

"What—what do you think you're doing?" she managed to squeak at last.

"Why, taking advantage of your somewhat blatant offer, of course," he responded as though she had just hung out a red light and a shingle.

"I didn't!" she protested indignantly.

"Sure you did," he murmured, dark head swooping and sensuous lips unerringly finding her startled ones.

Shock kept C.J. powerless in his embrace for long minutes, that and the strange quivering in her knees. She felt his mouth moving expertly on hers, his tongue probing with the stark thrust of possession, and a sudden heat enveloped her.

Her arms were beginning to creep up around his neck when sanity abruptly asserted itself. Oh, for heaven's sake—! She twisted suddenly, escaping his hold and ducking under his arm to retreat to the middle of the room. "Get out of here!" she ordered, hearing with a small astonishment the breathlessness in her voice.

He turned and came toward her, a peculiar

little smile lifting the corners of his mouth. "Don't be ridiculous."

She retreated another step and cast a harried glance toward the phone by her bed. "I'll call the manager."

"You can't reach the phone," he taunted softly, still coming toward her. "Not without going through me."

Panicked, C.J. took another step backward and came up against the bed. Her eyes widening, she said quickly, "I'll scream," and opened her mouth to do just that.

And then, suddenly, she was falling back on the bed with the stranger for company. He caught most of his own weight on his elbows, but C.J. nonetheless had the sensation of having the breath knocked from her.

Staring down into shocked tawny eyes, the stranger said solemnly, "Little girls shouldn't invite strange men into their bedrooms. Especially beautiful little girls with copper hair and tawny eyes and a smile like Venus herself. It's just not safe."

C.J. was suddenly, burningly aware that this man had been having a bit of fun at her expense. "I'm not a little girl!" she snapped. "And get off me!"

He rolled away to sit on the edge of the bed, grinning now. And that grin, C.J. noted unwillingly, softened his stern Indian-face into something charming and strangely endearing. With a shock of black hair falling over his forehead, he looked like a playful little boy.

She shoved the impression aside and raised herself on her elbows, glaring at him irritably. "Do you want an explanation now?"

"The timing seems right for it," he murmured, but held up a hand when she would have begun.

"Wait. Strangers should be introduced. I'm Fate Weston."

"You'd have to be," she muttered. *Fate*, for heaven's sake!

"I beg your pardon?" His lurking grin showed that he'd heard her quite clearly.

"Nothing. I'm C.J. Adams."

"What does the C.J. stand for?"

"None of your business."

"Oh." He didn't seem noticeably dashed. "Well, on with the story."

C.J. toyed with the idea of throwing something at him after the somewhat mocking remark. Since nothing was within reach, she contented herself with deepening her glare. It didn't seem to bother him, so she sighed and explained the situation. She went rather more into detail than she'd planned, mainly because Fate inserted a question now and then, and she answered automatically.

She explained that they were here in Aspen for Kathy's wedding, that they'd be joined on Friday (barring a blizzard) by four husbands and one fiancé. She provided thumbnail sketches of her friends, and the matchmaking which had caused her to pull a stranger from the hallway and invent a spur-of-the-moment, mysterious romance.

Feeling more and more like a fool—an unfamiliar sensation—she silently blamed her impulse on sheer insanity and hoped that he'd leave so that she could go soak in the bathtub and quietly drown herself.

Fate didn't laugh at her, however, but listened gravely. "So you wanted to teach your friends a lesson and get them off your back," he summed up when she had finished.

"Something like that," she said, and moved around to sit on the foot of the bed. She intended to tell him politely that since he had his explanation he could leave now, but he didn't give her the chance.

Getting to his feet, he paced slowly over to the window, slanted brows drawn together in a thoughtful frown. "This," he said consideringly, "is going to take careful planning."

"What is?" she asked blankly.

Fate turned to look at her, propping his shoulder against the window frame. "Our romance, of course," he said solemnly.

C.J. said the first thing that came to mind. "Are you crazy?"

"Now, darling," he said reproachfully, "you shouldn't say things like that to your one true love!"

"You . . . you . . ." she sputtered ineffectually.

Fate went on as though she were listening eagerly. "There has to be some reason why you've been hiding me all this time. Star-crossed lovers? Maybe I have a wife somewhere. . . . No, that wouldn't make you look too good, would it? Or me either."

"If you think—"

"Parental disapproval? No, we're both a little old for that. At least—How old are you, by the way?"

"Twenty-six. You—"

"Well, I'm thirty-four, so that disposes of the parental disapproval bit. How about a conflict of interests? What do you do for a living?"

"I'm a research librarian. I'm not going to—"

"I'm a lawyer. I don't see any conflict there, do you? Unless you don't like rough winters—I work in Denver. . . . But that can't be because you're here in Aspen."

C.J. took a deep breath and, tired of being interrupted, spent a good five minutes swearing at him in half a dozen languages, using words her professors never taught her. She even came up with a lovely medieval insult, and then capped off the whole with some choice gutter French.

And even in the midst of her tirade, she was astonished at herself. C.J. didn't swear. Her friends would have been stunned to hear such words coming from their quiet, inoffensive C.J.—particularly since none of them had been able to rouse her to temper after twenty years of needling.

Fate Weston had accomplished the feat in a little less than twenty minutes, with no effort at all.

In spite of her red hair, she was a very even-tempered woman—or had been up to now. In twenty-six years, her most violent anger had taken the form of mild irritation.

Until now.

Fate listened with twitching lips to her tirade, then asked interestedly, "How many languages do you speak?"

"Six," she replied from between clenched teeth.

"That's fascinating. But, back to the romance. Why haven't you introduced me to your friends? They're going to ask, you know. And we have to come up with a reasonable, logical—"

"There's nothing even remotely reasonable or logical about this farce! And no matter what you may be thinking right now, I did not come here to provide entertainment for bored lawyers!"

Fate folded his arms across his chest and smiled gently at her. "Then what will you tell your friends?"

C.J. opened and closed her mouth a few times, then said triumphantly, "I'll tell them we had a lovers' quarrel and broke up!"

"And don't you think," he suggested mildly, "that your friends "will try to get us back together again?"

She could feel the threads of the tangled web slowly drawing her in. He was absolutely right— damn him! "Then I—I'll tell them I made the whole thing up," she managed weakly.

"And be teased unmercifully for the rest of your vacation about accosting strange men in hall-ways?"

Two

Even with only thumbnail sketches of her friends, Fate had managed to put his finger right on the crux of the problem. C.J. would have been willing to do almost anything to avoid more teasing from her friends. After twenty years, she was thoroughly fed up with that. And only just realizing it.

She rubbed her forehead fretfully. "Oh Lord, how did I get myself into this mess?" she moaned hopelessly.

"Spilled milk," he murmured. "But since you *are* in this mess, the least I can do is help you out of it. Now, how did you and I meet? They're bound to ask that."

"I don't know!" she wailed, glaring at him. "You're not helping, C.J."

"Look, this is not going to work! I can't pretend that I'm in love with you—I don't even know you!" Something inside C.J. gave a little quiver as she realized that she was actually considering the idea . . . seriously.

Smiling oddly, he said, "You did a pretty good

job of pretending out in the hall." He obviously enjoyed her confusion, then went on in a reasonable, matter-of-fact tone. "It shouldn't be any problem for either of us, I think. All of you will be pretty busy getting ready for that wedding on Saturday, so we won't have to spend much time together this week, especially after your friends' husbands arrive. So all we have to do is to appear together from time to time and hold hands or something, then disappear and trust everyone to be nice and tactful."

"They won't be," C.J. said wearily, her thoughts chasing one another in panicky circles as she tried to come up with another way out of this mess. "You don't know my friends. They'll ask questions. And *questions*. And they won't rest until they know the whole truth. I won't have a moment's peace and neither will you; believe me, they won't be the slightest bit reticent about questioning you."

Fate didn't seem daunted by the prospect. "Then we'll have to get our story straight, won't we?" He sat down in a chair near the foot of the bed and smiled at her.

C.J. looked at him for the first time with real curiosity. "Why are you doing this? I mean, you could simply leave me to sink or swim and not bother."

"Would you believe love at first sight?" he asked with a hopeful expression.

"Not hardly," she responded dryly.

"Oh. Well . . . let's just say that I'm a frustrated actor at heart. Most lawyers are, you know."

C.J. had the curious impression that he was laughing at her . . . but kindly. As if there were some private joke concerning her that he wanted her to see for herself. Maybe it was that odd little smile she kept glimpsing.

Without the slightest bit of self-consciousness, she stared at his face thoughtfully. Although she certainly had noticed his good looks, things had been happening too rapidly for her to really take in the individual features. Curious about what sort of man would throw himself cheerfully into the small deception of a woman he'd never meet before, she studied him now.

If character was truly revealed in one's face—and C.J. had never been completely comfortable with that theory—then Fate Weston had a great deal of it. His mobile mouth was not only sensual, but filled with humor. There were faint laugh lines at the corners of his dark eyes which added to the impression of humor, and she was almost positive she'd seen an elusive dimple in one lean cheek.

Point one, then: the man possessed a sense of humor.

The dark eyes gazed calmly back at her as she thoughtfully considered these supposed windows to the soul. Heavy-lidded, intelligent, and perfectly capable of concealment, she mused silently. There was a native shrewdness in them which told her that this man hadn't needed college or a law degree to be considered intelligent. She found herself wondering exactly what color they were. Blue? She peered a bit more intently. No—purple. How odd! Deep, velvety purple. She filed the information away.

Point two: he was intelligent and wouldn't reveal his thoughts unless he chose to.

Unaware of the silence which had descended upon the room, C.J. continued her scrutiny, still without self-consciousness.

His jaw was firm without being overly aggressive, his chin slightly stubborn but not obstinate. The set of his head told her that he was proud—perhaps even arrogant. Bone structure was very good: strong, well-molded, creating stark planes and angles which were striking at first glance . . . and fascinating with each succeeding glance. A solemn Indian-face, turned to boyishness with a smile.

Point three: he was very attractive, and probably perfectly well aware of that fact.

Her eyes glided over the relaxed body in the chair. Having come into rather abrupt contact with that body, she could attest to its muscled firmness. If he wasn't an athlete, then he certainly took good care of himself.

Which only added to point three.

And when all three points came together, they added up to something which quite easily could turn a woman's world upside down before she could grab something to hold on to.

C.J. was startled at the unquestionably feminine thought, and even more startled when her tawny eyes slid back up Fate's body and came into contact with his purple gaze. There was an unsettling warmth in those eyes, along with a faint question.

She looked away hastily, shaken without knowing why and fighting a bewildering sudden, unfamiliar urge to reach out and touch him. She had never been so aware of another person in her life, and it gave her a strangely naked, vulnerable feeling. A feeling that she didn't like at all.

"Satisfied?" Fate asked softly.

"I don't know what you mean." C.J.'s eyes skittered across the room and collided with her reflection in the mirror. The tawny eyes staring back at her were feverish, oddly shocked. Unfamiliar eyes that belonged to someone else.

"With the inventory," he elaborated a bit dryly,

and then went on briskly, "Facts, Miss Adams, we need facts. Now, where could we have met?"

C.J. made a desperate effort to pull herself together, and forced her gaze to meet his calmly. Every instinct she possessed—latent feminine instincts neither needed nor wanted until now—warned her not to play any kind of game with this man. But the warning was a challenge in itself, and C.J. never refused a challenge.

And that lifelong pull of the new and exciting quite suddenly made up C.J.'s mind for her. Her mental warning wasn't the only challenge floating around in the room at the moment; there was also a coolly amused, half-mocking challenge in the purple depths of Fate's eyes. Sparks of gold defiance glittered in her eyes unconsciously as she met the challenge halfway.

"You don't seem to see the pitfalls looming in front of us," she warned. "I'm what's known as a 'studious' person." She hated the word, and offered it with a faint grimace. "My friends and I have known one another practically since the year one. It won't be easy to convince them that I've been having a romantic fling or whatever in the study room of the library."

His lips twitched slightly in that way which was beginning to fascinate her.

"What about vacations?"

"We've spent every vacation since high school together."

"What a chummy group," he remarked. Before she could respond, he went on easily. "Well, then, let's come up with some period during which we *could* have met. A romance such as ours . . . two months, I'd say. Where were you two months ago?"

C.J. thought for a moment, getting interested in his plotting in spite of herself. "Two months ago, I was at a librarian's conference in New York."

He brightened. "Terrific! At the same time, I was in New York on business. And I stayed at your hotel. Now, how did we actually meet?" He paused, then grinned at her. "Pity we can't at least be truthful about our meeting—that's one experience I'll treasure for years!"

C.J. flushed and glared at him briefly. Then, sighing, she got up and walked around to the side of the bed. Glancing his way, she was faintly surprised at his sudden stillness, the watchful eyes, but paid little atttention to it. Since his plotting was obviously going to take a while, she stretched out on the bed on her stomach, head at the foot of the bed, and propped her chin in her hands. "Go on, Maestro . . . how did we meet?"

An odd little sigh came from Fate, almost unconsciously it seemed. Very softly, he said, "Thought you were going to call the manager for a minute there, pixie."

C.J. felt a flush creeping up her cheeks, and hoped devoutly that her fingers hid the evidence that she'd never even considered it. "Oh, darn," she managed to say regretfully, "missed my chance." Judging by the glint in his dark eyes, he wasn't deceived, but Fate ruthlessly turned the conversation back to the original topic.

"Let's say we were introduced by a mutual friend." He steepled his fingers over his lean waist and stared at them thoughtfully. "How does that sound?"

"Fishy. I don't have many friends in New York."

"One will do," he pointed out patiently.

"Touché," she said with a reluctant sigh.

"Okay. We tumbled headlong into love and had a passionate week."

"Weekend. I was only in New York for the weekend."

"That's not very much time," he protested, wounded.

"Sorry, Maestro. But Jan knows when I got home, because I had dinner with her and Brian."

"Now why the hell did you have to do that? You're ruining my chain of events!"

Amused, she said again, "Sorry. But how was I to know I'd be called upon to have time to fall in love?"

Fate lifted an eyebrow at her and reflected. "Well . . . what the hell. We had a passionate weekend. Threw caution to the wind. Became so engrossed in each other—"

Before he could warm further to his theme—as he showed every sign of doing—she interrupted to say practically, "But I was busy with the conference both days. I barely had time to eat, much less—"

"You're just not entering into the spirit of this, C.J.," he interrupted in an aggrieved voice. "Your friends weren't—I hope—with you, so they don't know what you did."

"That's true," she said, reluctantly. "So we had a passionate weekend. Then what, Maestro?"

"We parted," he answered with great relish. "Tearing out our souls in agony."

"If it tore out our souls to part," she said, regarding him with utter fascination, "then why did we?"

He waved a hand with grand impatience. "We'll get to that later. Here comes one of the sticky places: how did we manage to keep this powerful love of ours aflame for two months? Passionate phone calls and stolen weekends?"

"Passionate phone calls, maybe. But stolen weekends—" She broke off abruptly and frowned. "Wait a minute. There *have* been three weekends since the conference that I've been out of town.

Some business with my father's estate . . . and I went to visit my sister . . . and an old professor invited me to stay with him and his wife while I was using some of his rare books for research."

"*Now* you're getting the hang of it. By the way—you didn't happen to call up one of your friends during those weekends, I hope?"

C.J. looked surprised. "No. But what would it matter if I had?"

He shook his head pityingly. "People engaging in passionate, stolen weekends don't call up their friends to chat. I have it on the best of authority."

C.J. didn't probe. "I'll bet. Keep spinning, Maestro; the web's nearly complete."

His lips twitched again, and again she watched with fascination. "Now for the second of the three sticky points," he said wryly. "Why didn't you tell your friends about me? If you're so close? Or are you the secretive type, cherishing love quietly in your heart and unwilling to lose the magic?"

She frowned at him. "That doesn't sound like me at all. Not that I'd shout it from the rooftops, but I would tell my friends. *Especially* since they've been matchmaking for years."

"There is that." He frowned. "Well, we'll just have to tie up the secrecy in the reason we tore out our souls."

"What?" she asked somewhat blankly.

"The reason we can't be together always," he explained patiently. "The reason we parted in New York and had to settle for stolen weekends and passionate phone calls."

"Which is?" When he continued to stare at her, she said, "I can't wait to hear this one."

He sighed. "That's the third sticky point. And, at the moment, I can't think of a way to explain it."

Fate rose to his feet and began pacing the narrow walkway between the door and the window. C.J. allowed her eyes to follow him back and forth, feeling rather like a spectator at a tennis match. Against her better judgment—which didn't seem to be in control today, *anyway*—she found herself trying to think of some logical reason why they couldn't be together. Nothing occurred to her.

He halted at last by the window and turned to stare at her. "I can't think of a thing. We'll just have to look pained and refuse to discuss it."

"Jan will do everything in her power to worm it out of me," C.J. said despairingly. "She *always* roots out secrets. And Brian's a policeman!"

"So?" Fate looked amused.

"So Brian's taught her to think logically. At least as logically as she *can* think, being Jan. She won't rest until she knows exactly what's going on, Fate." C.J. used his name quite unconsciously for the first time, and missed the sudden gleam in his dark eyes because she was scrambling off the bed.

"We'll muddle through somehow," he said cryptically.

She pushed her hair off her forehead and glanced at the broad masculine watch on her wrist. "It's almost dinnertime. I'd better go face them and get it over with."

"Why don't we have dinner together," he suggested, moving slowly toward her. "We need more rehearsal time."

C.J. shook her head, not without a certain amount of regret. "They'll be hurt if I don't tell them something. You could be waiting in your room for a phone call or something—" She broke off and looked up at him guiltily. "I'm sorry. You probably have plans of your own. This is going to ruin your vacation!"

"If it does, I'll have only myself to blame, won't

I?" His lips twitched again in that odd, sup-
pressed smile C.J. found so completely fascinating.
He reached up, two large, warm hands framing
her face, a smothered, soft laugh escaping from
his lips. "Don't look so confused and nervous,
pixie. As adorable as it makes you look, I just
won't have it. We'll come through this with flying
colors—see if we don't."

Before C.J. could respond, he bent his head,
his lips touching hers so gently that it felt to her
like a sigh. A strangely shocking sigh. Over almost before it began.

Staring up at him with even more confusion in
her eyes as he drew back, she fought to keep her
voice steady, and to ignore the hands still framing
her face. "Why are you doing this?" she asked
again, wary, perplexed—and not sure whether she
was questioning his active participation in her
charade . . . or the kiss.

"I fell in love." His voice was whimsical, velvety
dark eyes caressing. "Apparently I do very strange
things when I fall in love with a beautiful pixie."
Without the slightest change in his tone, he added,
"You go and have dinner with your friends. I'll
make an appearance later for the first act of our
play."

C.J. found herself sinking back on her bed as
the door closed behind him. Her eyes connected
with her reflection in the mirror again, and again
she suffered shock. How strange she looked! A
not unbecoming flush lightly colored her cheeks,
and her eyes appeared huge and startingly bright.

Had he really said that she looked adorable?
And had he really called her beautiful? Twice?
Why was her heart thudding against her ribs like
a jungle drum gone mad? She felt both hot and
cold, and she was quivering from head to toe. And
the room suddenly felt very, very empty.

Oh, but he was good! He'd accepted with enthusiasm the role of lover, thrust upon him by her own reckless action. And he was absolutely perfect in the part. Practicing, that was all. Not that he needed it. He'd even practiced telling her that he loved her. And she had not the slightest doubt that her friends would believe that much, at least. That he loved her.

For one heart-stopping moment, she'd believed it herself.

And now she had to act as though she did believe it. She had to convince her friends that she was a woman in love. That realization sent panic bouncing around in her mind, adding to the confusion of Fate's effect on her senses.

She stared toward the door, tearing her gaze from the stranger in the mirror. Maestro. She'd called him Maestro. And he was a master in this particular art. The art of skillful deception. Pulling all the threads together to insure that the entire web didn't fall apart. And suddenly, she wished that she'd agreed to have dinner with him. Not because she wanted to, of course.

She needed more coaching from the master.

"Who am I fooling," she muttered despairingly to the empty room. "I couldn't act my way out of a paper bag. I couldn't act like I was drowning if I *was*. I couldn't act . . ."

She was still muttering to herself—rather like whistling in the dark—when she left her room. And she devoutly hoped that the stranger she'd seen in the mirror remained there. She didn't know that woman. She was afraid to know that woman.

That woman had the look of someone waking up. The look of a butterfly coming out of its cocoon, soft and vulnerable. And ready to test its wings for the very first time.

And, no . . . C.J. didn't want to see that woman again. Flying was a dangerous business. A scary, dangerous business. She wasn't ready to test her wings yet. Not yet . . .

As soon as she entered the huge, rustic dining room off the lobby, C.J. spotted her friends seated around a table in the far corner. She began threading her way through the crowded room, only dimly noting the pine-paneled walls dotted with paintings of snow-covered landscapes and the thick carpet beneath her feet.

Her insides felt like jelly, and panic had fogged her brain until she couldn't think at all. The only fact that kept dancing through her mind was that she was going to regret until her dying day her first impulsive, reckless action in twenty-six years.

She slid quickly into the empty chair at the table and smiled with what she devoutly hoped was gentle apology. "Sorry I'm late." She was astonished at how calm she sounded.

Immediately, she came under the battery of five pairs of eyes of various colors, holding identical expressions of lingering shock, disbelief, and not-so-quiet anger.

"C.J. Adams, *who* was that man, and why didn't you tell us about what is obviously a hot-and-heavy love affair?" Jan demanded irately.

C.J. all but jumped out of her chair, casting nervous glances at several nearby, startled diners. "Why don't you yell a little louder, Jan, and wake the dead?"

"Well, who is he, C.J.?" Ann asked softly. "You've never said a word about him!"

"She still hasn't said a word," Kathy offered flatly, tossing her auburn hair and aiming a challenging glare at C.J.

"You haven't given her a chance," Susan pointed out coolly.

When an expectant silence finally fell, C.J. toyed uneasily with her water glass and tried to remember the master's farcical story. "His name's Fate Weston," she managed at last, stubbornly refusing to meet anyone's eyes.

"Fate? What a marvelous name!" Tami bubbled.

Ignoring the interruption, C.J. went on firmly, determined to get the story over with. "He's a lawyer and he lives in Denver. We met two months ago—that weekend I was at the conference."

"What was a lawyer doing at a librarian's conference?" Jan asked skeptically.

"Nothing. I mean—he wasn't. He was just staying at the same hotel. A mutual friend introduced us and—and that's all there is to it." Her brief explanation wouldn't have mollified a curious three-year-old, and nobody knew that better than C.J.

Kathy was frowning at her. "C.J.—what about the last two months? If he lives in Denver, and you live in Boston, how've the two of you managed to meet? And when?"

C.J. was sorely tempted to say something soulful about stolen weekends and passionate phone calls, but didn't trust herself to. Striking a happy medium, she said vaguely, "There's Ma Bell, you know. And there were several weekends . . ."

"You *said* you were visiting your sister!" Tami exclaimed.

"And seeing to your father's estate," Jan added wryly.

"And doing research," Susan murmured.

"Now for the sixty-four-dollar question," Kathy put in, looking rather intently at C.J. "Why didn't you tell us?"

"There were reasons." C.J. was still trying desperately to come up with a few. "I didn't mean to hurt any of you, it's just that . . . there were reasons," she ended lamely.

Her friends weren't, of course, satisfied with that, but C.J. stuck to her non-explanation with unusual tenacity. During the next hour she got a great deal of practice in fielding unanswerable questions and talking without saying much. She devoted most of her attention to her meal and made vague replies to curious questions without looking up. Later, for the life of her, she couldn't recall what she had eaten.

Normally calm even in a crisis, she found her nerves growing more and more taut as the meal stretched interminably. She was still very much disturbed by the changes she was afraid Fate had brought into her life, and her friends' probing was only making matters worse.

Finally she felt she had pushed the food on her plate around enough, and escaped from the table with a few murmured words that could have been taken to mean anything. At the door of the dining room she realized with dismay that her stubborn friends were right behind her.

She wandered into the large lounge at the back of the building's ground floor, reluctant to escape to her room where the stranger in the mirror waited. She glanced at the comfortable chairs and divans placed in conversation-inspiring groupings around the two huge stone fireplaces in the room, and headed immediately for the warmth of a blazing fire.

"C.J., can't you tell us what the problem is? My God—we've known each other since we were snotty-nosed brats!"

"Is it something about *him*? Does he—Oh, C.J., does he have a wife or something?"

"Honey, you can tell us!"

"You look so strange, C.J.—not at all like yourself!"

Her friends.

Quite suddenly, her nerves stretched to the limit and snapped. Turning with the abrupt movement of someone who has to move or jump out of her skin, she exclaimed, "*Damnit*, will you just leave me alone!"

The silence was sudden and devastating. The girls couldn't have looked more shocked if she had pulled out a gun and threatened to shoot them. A part of C.J. wanted to laugh, but another part of her wanted to cry hysterically.

"I'm sorry." There was a wealth of bewilderment in her quivering voice. "I'm sorry. I don't know what's wrong with me . . ."

A hand gripped her arm just then, and C.J. turned with an instinct older than time to bury her face in the soft wool of a sweater. It wasn't until she was breathing in the tangy scent of Fate's cologne that she understood her body had known it was him. She had turned to him like a confused child seeking comfort and security.

Oh, God, what he must be thinking! Embarrassed by her abandoned gesture, she was nonetheless powerless to pull away from him; she just couldn't face her friends right then. She heard Fate speaking over her head, introducing himself to her friends, and then heard the voices of her friends returning the courtesy.

He had his arms around her, she realized dimly, and she felt her heart begin its thunderous knocking again. Oh, what was wrong with her? There were tears on her cheeks, wetting his sweater, and she didn't remember shedding them. What was wrong with her?

A large white handkerchief was thrust into her hands. They gravitated to the divan. She sat beside Fate, in the circle of his arm, automatically wiping her eyes with the handkerchief he had given her. Her friends were sitting in a little semicircle around them, watching her as though she were a total stranger.

Fate began speaking to them, and C.J. noted with relief that their attention turned immediately to him.

"You'll have to forgive her if she's seemed a bit distracted since I arrived," he told them with a grave smile. "You see, until then, she hadn't known why we couldn't be together."

"She didn't?" five voices exclaimed.

"I didn't?" Fortunately C.J.'s bewildered voice got lost among all the rest.

Fate's sheltering arm drew her a bit closer. "Poor darling—she's had a shock, I'm afraid. It was good news, but when she found out what I'd been keeping from her all this time . . ."

"And what was that?" Jan's suspicion was offset by definite interest.

"When we first met, I knew that C.J. was the only woman in the world for me. She looked up at me with those great yellow eyes . . . and I thought the building had fallen in on me. I wanted to tell her that I loved her, needed her desperately."

Fate's deep voice throbbed with such passionate sincerity that C.J. stared at him in utter astonishment. Rather hastily, he gathered her into his arms, one hand on her head firmly—and ruthlessly—pressing her face into the curve of his shoulder.

"But I had to let her go," he told his listeners thickly, holding C.J. in what looked like a desperately adoring embrace. "I just couldn't bear to tell her the truth . . ."

"What *was* the truth? What was wrong?" Jan's

voice had lost the suspicion and now held only sympathetic anxiety.

"I was in New York for tests . . . medical tests. I'd been told weeks before that I had only a few months left . . ."

"Oh, no!"

"You poor man!"

"And you couldn't tell C.J. How sad!"

"You mean you're—you're—?"

"Of course he isn't! He said it was *good* news."

Amazement warred with a powerful desire to burst out laughing as C.J. listened to Fate's absurd story. The tears of only moments before were gone and forgotten. She was incredulous that he thought himself able to get away with such a ridiculous tale, and dumbfounded to realize that he *was* getting away with it.

Her friends were not fools. Ann and Susan had graduated from Wellesley, and both Jan and Kathy had gone to Radcliffe—although neither had finished—with C.J. They were intelligent, well-read, well-traveled, very aware women.

But they were *buying* Fate's story.

And that, she knew, was due to his delivery. He was so obviously moved—so utterly convincing and so *damn* believable—that C.J. had to remind herself at least twice that it was all one big fat lie. She found herself beathing in the fine wool of his sweater, and realized suddenly that her mouth was hanging open. And no wonder!

She struggled to raise her head and stop the whole thing before her friends figured out that they were being led down the proverbial garden path, but Fate's strong hand kept her face hidden with vastly irritating ease.

"Don't cry, darling," he murmured soothingly into her hair as though she were sobbing her heart out. "It's all over now."

C.J. managed to work one hand around where the others couldn't see it and fiercely pinched the flesh over his ribs. She felt him jump slightly, but he went on talking as if nothing had happened.

And as he continued, C.J. began to make muffled choking sounds which probably sounded like crying. She only heard about half of what Fate told the girls, but that half alone made her feel desperately in need of someplace quiet and dark where she could laugh herself silly.

Apparently, he'd picked up some kind of wild, rare parasite in Egypt (*Egypt*?) months before, and then came back to the States to be told that the bug was going to kill him. No cure. No hope. An experimental treatment being offered in New York had been his only hope. A treatment with . . . laser beams.

Laser beams? *Laser beams*? For two solid months, laser beams and parasites had warred within his frail body. It was a wonder he didn't light up a dark room all by himself. Clinging hopelessly to his love for C.J., he'd borne the painful, nauseating treatments in brave silence. With a nobility which would have done credit to a saint, he'd hidden the truth from her, sustaining himself on the rare phone calls and stolen weekends they shared. They couldn't be together, he'd explained to a wonderfully trusting C.J., but he couldn't tell her why. He could only tell her that he needed her desperately.

Poor man. His body ravaged by parasites and bombarded by laser beams. In love for the first time in his life and doomed to lose that love. Stoically enduring the constant mental and physical pain. Hoping against hope that the bugs would give up and vacate.

And then, finally, being told that the treatments had been a success. Rushing here to tell C.J. it had been her love that had cured him. The love they were now free to shout to the world . . .

He didn't tell the story quite that way, of course. In some peculiar way, he made it believable.

C.J. heard sniffs and admiring murmurs from her friends, and vaguely pondered the gullibility of women being charmed by a handsome lawyer/actor who had obviously never had a sick day in his life. But she kept her face hidden against his shoulder, needing no urging at all from him now.

The wide grin on her face would have ruined his story.

Three

"Civil or criminal?"

C.J. was sitting on her bed in her room, exactly where Fate had set her after carrying her all the way from the lounge—accompanied by her friends as far as the door. She was staring at the fiend who was leaning against her dresser and gazing at her with a gleam of unholy laughter in his purple eyes.

"I beg your pardon?" One slanted brow rose questioningly.

"Your profession. Law." C.J. managed to hold on to her expressionless tone with a tremendous effort. "Civil or criminal?"

"Criminal," he answered.

"That explains it." She took a deep breath, and added in a refined scream, "You've been associating with degenerates too long!"

"I'm a defense attorney, pixie; I don't consider my clients degenerates."

C.J. ignored the information. "You're not playing with a full deck, do you know that? Your pilot light's gone out. All the sand's sifted through your bucket. You don't have both oars in the water!"

"Are you trying to say I'm crazy?"

"I'm not *trying* to say it, I'm *saying* it! Oh, I'll bet the men in the little white coats are looking for you."

"I gave them the slip in Denver," he said.

"*Laser beams*? To treat parasites?"

"What *will* they think of next?"

C.J. buried her face in her hands, a muffled growl of frustration escaping from between her fingers. Then she started laughing. She laughed so long and hard that her throat hurt.

When she finally lifted her face, tears of laughter sparkled in her eyes. Not even her intense, growing awareness of this man could hold the amusement at bay. Realizing that she was still clutching his handkerchief, she waved it like a flag of surrender.

"I give up! Maestro, my compliments. I have no doubt that you sold my friends on your unbelievable, ridiculous, utterly absurd story."

The fiend had turned into a mischievous little boy. A grin slashed across his dark face, revealing even white teeth. Modestly, he said, "Like I always say—if you're going to tell a lie, make it a whopper!"

"Uh huh." She choked on another laugh. "God, I thought I was going to die. And *you*, you monster, shoving my face into your sweater like that! I could barely breathe!"

"Sorry, pixie, but I had to do something fast. Your face was a dead giveaway."

Suddenly aware that he'd carried her all the way from the lounge without even a token protest from her, C.J. felt her face growing hot. She told herself that she could hardly have protested with her friends dogging Fate's heels, but that was small comfort. She had an awful feeling that, given an opportunity, she would have remained silent.

Hastily repairing the omission, she said severely, "You shouldn't have carried me all that way. It was completely unnecessary."

"Like I said, your expression would have given the show away," he responded, unrepentant. He studied her flushing face with interest. "You look cute as hell when you're embarrassed."

"What makes you think I'm embarrassed?" she fired up immediately.

"You're blushing."

"I am not!"

"Then you're running a fever. Your face is a very fetching shade of pink."

C.J. fought an impulse to peer past him into the mirror. "I am not running a fever," she gritted out. "And I'm not blushing, either. If my face is red, it's only because I'm absolutely furious. How *dare* you tell such a story to my friends!"

"You thought it was funny a minute ago," he pointed out.

"Well, it isn't now." She swallowed a last giggle and tried to keep the glare on her face. "They'll have you drawn and quartered when they find out the truth, and I shudder to think what they'll do to me!"

"There's no reason why they have to find out the truth," he said easily. "So we're both safe."

"Of course they'll find out," she retorted irritably. "When this never-to-be-sufficiently-regretted vacation is over and we go our separate ways, they'll figure out it was all a sham!"

Very gently, he said, "You weren't listening to my story very closely downstairs, pixie."

"Stop calling me that!" she snapped and then added, as curiosity got the better of her, "What *did* you say to them?"

"I set the date."

"The date?" C.J. ran a bewildered hand through her copper curls and stared at him. "The date for what?"

For all the world as though he were discussing the possibility of snow, Fate replied casually, "The date for our wedding."

Assuming that he was joking, she exclaimed, "Did you *have* to add that little bit to the story, for heaven's sake? I'll look like an utter fool when I'm left at the altar!"

"But you won't be left at the altar."

The deep, gentle voice slowly sank into C.J.'s brain as she blinked at him a couple of times. There was no longer a trace of little-boy mischief in his dark eyes, she realized. He looked serious, grave.

He meant it.

For a split second, a surge of unfamiliar, unidentifiable emotion blocked her throat. But then the unreality of the situation came to her rescue. And the C.J. she knew, slightly cynical, not at all naïve, came rapidly to the fore.

"It's customary," she informed him calmly, "to ask."

"True." He rubbed the bridge of his nose with a thoughtful frown. "The thing is, you see—if I ask, you'll only turn me down. You haven't known me long enough to appreciate my sterling qualities. And I can't bear rejection."

She smiled sweetly. "You'll have to learn to."

"Oh, I don't think so. Your friends are no doubt already planning the wedding, pixie. We're due to marry on Valentine's Day."

"How romantic," she said evenly.

"I thought so."

"It won't happen."

"Of course it will. You have a whole month to get used to the idea."

"You're being ridiculous, of course."

He smiled. "No. Just going after what I want."

"Meaning that you want me?"

"Of course." He straightened, a gleam in his dark eyes. "I'll be glad—more than happy—to show you just how much I want you."

Rather hastily, she said, "I'll take it as read!"

With unflattering speed, he resumed his lounging posture against the dresser. "Suit yourself."

C.J. wondered why she suddenly wanted to throw something heavy at him. Determined to keep things as light as possible under the circumstances, she said dryly, "*You're* going to look a little silly standing all alone at the altar."

His grin was a charming, rueful thing to watch. "I've sized up your friends pretty well, I think. If I don't manage to talk you into marrying me, they'll deliver you to the church anyway—bound and gagged if necessary."

Cynical C.J. decided to employ brutal tactics. "Why," she asked starkly, "do you want to marry me?"

"Natural progression," he answered solemnly. "With this burning love affair behind us, marriage is obligatory."

She chewed that one over for a moment or so, then lifted a wry brow at him. "You mean you gave my friends a date just to make your tale seem more convincing?"

"No," he said gently, "I gave them a date because I intend to marry you. On Valentine's Day."

C.J. decided quite sanely that she was probably tired enough to be imagining things. *Had* to be. No man proposed to a woman after a mere six hours' acquaintance. "I can't deal with you tonight," she said. "Go away."

A gleam of laughter lit his eyes at the irritable dismissal, but he made no move to leave her. "I haven't been here long enough. As a matter of fact, I shouldn't leave here at all."

"What?" She was so tired that her voice emerged almost mild.

He looked thoughtful. "Correct me if I'm wrong, but doesn't—Jan, is it?—have the room next to this one? The tall blonde?"

C.J. nodded. "Yes, Jan's next door. Why?"

"Because as convincing as my whopper was"—he bowed modestly—"I don't think that Jan quite believed it."

"She sounded as if she did. What makes you think she didn't?"

"Well . . . you certainly know her better than I do. But I've had a lot of practice watching the faces of a jury. Jan is suspicious. She said all the right words and made all the right noises . . . and she's going to be watching us like a hawk."

"So?" C.J. just didn't see the point.

Dryly, he told her, "A man and woman having a passionate love affair don't sleep in separate rooms. And Jan's probably listening to find out when I leave."

This time, the point sank in. "You are not spending the night in my room," she managed at last.

"I have to," he explained patiently. "To preserve the charade. But I'll creep out by dawn's light to keep your reputation intact."

C.J. thought longingly of the not-so-distant past when she had been wrapped in abstraction and safe from situations like this. "No. You're not staying here." She took a deep breath. "If six hours of pretense does this to me, I'll be a basket case by the end of next week. I'm telling the girls the truth in the morning. Goodbye."

He chuckled softly. "As simple as that, huh?"

"That's right."

"You must be tired if you think it's that simple. If you tell them the truth, we'll both look like fools."

"At this point, I don't particularly care."

In a coolly mocking tone, he said, "So you're going to do the cowardly thing. You don't believe that you have the ability to carry off a simple charade; you can't act like a woman in love. So you'll tell your friends it was all a lie, and be safely back in character."

For some reason, his comments stung, and C.J. had an uneasy feeling that he'd planned it that way. Defensively she told him, "It's the only sensible thing to do! I've never been a very good liar, and I don't want to start now."

"You're a coward," he insisted softly, flatly.

"It isn't cowardly to tell the truth!"

"It's cowardly to start something and not follow through."

"Not if what you started was a deception!"

He was silent for a moment, studying her with the curiously veiled purple eyes. Then, calmly, he told her, "I threw down the gauntlet, pixie, and you picked it up. You're not about to let me win by default."

Instantly, C.J. knew that he meant the challenge she'd seen in his eyes hours before. Recklessness surged through her yet another time, but this time she managed to keep a tight rein on it. "You win," she said lightly. "By default."

Musingly he said, "And what if I tell the girls you're lying?"

"They won't believe you."

"No, they won't. But they won't be able to understand the situation. Here's a total stranger playing the lover and insisting that you and he have been having a passionate love affair for two months.

He's bewildered and dejected because the woman he loves is claiming they don't even know one another. And after she greeted him so happily, too! Of course, he'll ask her friends what's wrong, and enlist their aid to straighten out everything. And of course—"

"They will!" C.J. finished bitterly, glaring at him. Jan may not have totally believed his story, she thought despairingly, but the others had. And they would think it just like their C.J. to panic and deny everything. The romance of a love affair would have fascinated C.J., and her friends knew it. But if Fate had truly "set the date," her friends would also believe that the thought of marriage had panicked her.

She could see the whole vacation before her like a nightmare. Whether or not her friends believed her denials, they'd still do everything in their collective power to shove her down the aisle.

"Let the play begin," Fate murmured in a satisfied tone, obviously seeing her thoughts written on her face. "You're damned if you do and damned if you don't, pixie. Might as well take the easy way out and enjoy your courtship."

"And get married on Valentine's Day," she finished dryly.

"Sure."

C.J. wasn't the slightest bit worried about an actual wedding taking place. In two weeks, she'd be safely back in Boston, working for her doctorate. All this would seem like a bad dream.

"Well? Do you agree that my way is best?"

She wondered dimly if she were imagining the tension she sensed within him. Why was he so determined to carry through with this ridiculous charade? Pushing the useless speculation away, she said evenly, "I'll agree to the charade. But it stops when the vacation stops."

For a moment, he seemed about to protest, but then he seemed to see the utter determination on her face. A peculiar smile creased his lean face, and something mischievous stirred in the purple eyes. "All right. The . . . charade . . . ends in two weeks."

C.J. gave a little sigh of relief. No more talk of marriage, then. But she wondered at his hesitation before and after the word "charade." Her victory had an oddly hollow feeling.

"So I have to spend the night here," he pointed out.

Determined not to act like this was the first time she'd ever entertained a man in her bedroom—even though it was—C.J. managed an unconcerned smile. "Fine." She gestured to the two uncomfortably modern chairs flanking the window. "Hope you'll be comfortable."

He sighed. "I was afraid you were going to say that."

"It's your choice—the chairs, the floor, or your own room." She got up. "Excuse me."

Bowing to her polite words, he moved aside so that she could get her sleeping gear from the dresser. "I don't suppose," he murmured in a wistful tone, "that I could convince you to share the bed? With a pillow between us?"

"Not even with the Berlin Wall between us," she said, and was startled at the grimness of her own voice.

A sudden laugh escaped him, as though in surprise. "Is the courtship getting to you already?" he demanded with a theatrical leer.

Not rising to the bait, she said, "I sleep alone," and felt faintly uncomfortable at the primness she heard. Before he could say anything else, she hastily unearthed the oversized green football jersey she slept in, and added, "I'm taking a shower and going to bed. It's been a long day. You're on your own."

He didn't say another word, but watched with veiled eyes as she headed for the bathroom. C.J. took her shower in a weary state of semiconsciousness. She didn't think because she didn't want to think. Tomorrow, when her mind was fresh, she'd sit down and figure out what was going on. And then she'd probably call somebody and have this lunatic hauled away. But tonight, she seemed to be stuck with him.

The stranger C.J. had seen in the mirror earlier—and felt within herself—had apparently gone back into hiding. But she surfaced with bewildering suddenness when C.J. came out of the bathroom to confront the "lover" in her bedroom.

He had slid the two chairs together near the foot of the bed with the folding luggage rack between them, making a peculiar-looking sort of lounge-cum-bed. His sweater had been discarded and lay over the back of the chair his feet were propped on, his shoes were neatly by the dresser. A blanket and pillow had been abstracted from the bed. He was looking perfectly comfortable, hands linked together behind his neck and white shirt unbuttoned halfway down his chest.

The room was suddenly shrinking around C.J.

Tugging at the white piping at the bottom of the thigh-length football jersey, she found her eyes skittering away from his steady gaze as she approached the bed. She could feel his sweeping look, and tugged again at the jersey. She became aware of her heart thudding again, and silently cursed the stranger who occupied her body in this bewildering way.

"Goodnight, pixie."

She jumped at the husky sound of his voice and, finding that there was no graceful way to slide into bed wearing a jersey, opted for speed over grace. "Goodnight," she muttered, reaching swiftly to turn out the lamp on the nightstand.

Lying still in bed with the covers pulled up to her chin, she listened to her heart pound and stared into darkness.

"Cynthia Jean," he murmured suddenly.

Baffled, she frowned at the darkness. "Having sweet dreams?" she asked him quizzically.

"Trying to figure out what the C.J. stands for," he responded in a musing voice. "Cynthia Jean?"

"No." She couldn't help but smile, feeling wide awake and amused by the guessing game that so many others had played.

"Carly Jo?"

"Sorry."

"Catherine Joanna?"

"Wrong again."

"Constance Julia?"

"Nope."

His sigh reached her easily. "I'll ask your friends in the morning. They'll take pity on me."

"Want to bet?"

"I've never met a woman yet who could keep a secret."

"You shouldn't make blanket statements." She giggled softly. "My friends and I have known each other for twenty years, but they've only known my name for eight years. It was my graduation present to them when we all finished high school. And since their own husbands haven't gotten it out of them, I doubt that you will."

"It must be a dilly of a name."

"Why else do you think I've had it stricken from every record except my birth certificate?" she asked wryly.

"Mmmm. Something exotic, then. Cleopatra Jacqueline?"

She choked on another giggle. "No, thank heavens. My mother wasn't deranged, just groggy from the anesthetic."

"So when she really woke up, she decided to call you C.J.?"

C.J. was silent for a moment. "No. My uncle did. I was called by my first name until I was four. Then my parents were killed in a plane crash, and my sister and I were raised by my father's brother."

"I'm sorry, pixie." His voice was sober.

"Don't be." There was a smile in her own voice. "I can barely remember them. And John was very good to Siri and me."

"John?"

"My uncle." She laughed softly. "He taught us never to call him 'Uncle John.' Said it made him feel old."

"Siri is your sister?"

"Yes. Another unusual name. And, before you ask, it isn't short for anything. My father just liked the sound of it."

"It was his turn to do the naming, huh?"

"After the disaster of my name, he wasn't taking any chances."

"It can't be that bad."

"It can. And is."

"Now you've got me on my mettle. I'll have to figure it out."

"Be my guest." C.J. smothered a yawn with her hand. "But I'm going to sleep."

"I'm not sleepy," he protested.

"Tough." She turned on her side, realizing only as she did so that she was facing him. "Sleep waits for no man. Goodnight."

"Let's play twenty questions," he suggested.

"No."

"Then I'll tell you a story."

"You've told too many stories today. Goodnight."

"But—"

"*Goodnight!*"

With a heavy sigh, Fate lapsed into silence. C.J. lay and listened to her travel clock ticking softly.

As Jan had pointed out earlier, C.J. had been working hard for months—too hard for too many months. She tended to push herself hard whenever she was working toward a goal, the self-imposed pace tiring her more than she realized. It caught up with her occasionally; yearly vacations were very necessary to her, and long hours of sleep were usually needed to recharge her energies.

The deep sleep C.J. slipped into was not unusual. Normally a light sleeper, there were infrequent nights such as this one when she experienced an almost coma-like unconsciousness. Very little would rouse her from the peculiar state. Deep, dreamless, totally relaxed, she might have been light-years away from the world.

But this night's sleep was different. She dreamed. C.J. was aware that she was dreaming, vaguely puzzled by it, but knew she wouldn't be able to wake herself up. The dream was odd, though, and seemed very, very real.

Purple stars were shining down at her, purple stars with exciting promises in them. C.J. didn't know how she understood the promises, but they were very clear to her. Purple promises bright with a challenge she'd never grow tired of. She wanted to lose herself in the stars, throw herself into them and become the heart of an exploding sun.

And there was an Indian somehow inside the stars, calling to her softly to come with him, to take his hand and become a part of him. His voice was the low rumble of a storm, his black hair flying in solar winds. The gray light of morning gave his form a striking silhouette and made her ache inside at his beauty.

Strong, sun-browned hands tenderly drew away the hazy clouds covering her body, the purple stars becoming eyes that saw her in a way she'd never been seen before. She reached out a hand to touch the Indian's face wonderingly, feeling the warm strength of it beneath her fingers and aching even more because he wasn't—couldn't be—real. He was carved from her dream.

Lips like rough velvet brushed her wrist, slid down her inner arm with torturing slowness. She turned her face aside as the lips reached her shoulder, sacrificing the sight of the Indian's face for the feeling of the lips on her throat.

She felt his thick, soft hair beneath her fingers, and stroked the darkness lovingly. Her other hand found a muscled shoulder and molded the smooth flesh with a need beyond reason. The heavy weight of him bore her down into the cloud beneath her back, and she absorbed this new sensation with delight.

He was whispering sweet, magical words to her in many languages, his breath warm in her ear. Telling her that he adored her, that she was beautiful and wonderful. Telling her that she was the other half of himself.

Kisses fell on her closed eyelids, no heavier than snowflakes, and she heard her soft voice pleading with him until his lips found hers with devastating need. Ignited by the flames in him, her body took fire, burning and torturing her with its aching emptiness.

She twined her arms around the strong column of his neck, her body arching beneath the wonderful weight that trapped her. Willing but inexperienced lips returned the raw desire of his mouth, her tongue exploring fervently.

She felt one of his hands surround a throbbing breast, and a moan ripped its way from the depths of her being. Sparks of light cartwheeled wildly behind her closed eyelids and a roaring filled her ears. When his lips left hers, she felt bereaved, adrift and alone. But he held her close, his hands gently stroking her back, lightly touching her face. Soothing. Calming.

A soft, beloved voice rumbled adoring promises. He'd take care of her, never leave her. She would walk by his side always.

Gradually, the nearly painful tension drained from her body. She clung to him, fearing that the dream was near its end and reluctant to lose this special closeness. Eyes firmly closed, she begged him wistfully to take her with him when he went back to the purple stars. He laughed softly, ruefully it seemed. Promised to return.

The dream was slipping away, and C.J. fought desperately to hold on to it. His deep voice was growing fainter, darkness was closing in on her. The purple stars were the last image in her mind, bright with the promises she'd heard. And then even they dimmed, and she realized sadly that she was alone again. Tears flooded her eyes and wet the cloud as she turned her face into it in despair. . . .

Her bedroom was filled with sunlight when C.J. at last opened her eyes and reluctantly greeted the day. She sat up, stretching and yawning. Staring toward the two chairs neatly flanking the window, a blanket and pillow placed on one of them, she wondered what was wrong with the scene. And then she remembered.

Fate.

Breaking off in mid-yawn, she stared warily around the room. It was empty. Turning to look at her travel clock, she felt her eyes widen in surprise. Well, no wonder he was gone; it was nearly noon. She'd slept half around the clock.

Remembering his penchant for tall tales and his promise to talk to the girls today, C.J. felt suddenly very uneasy. The girls were early risers and she was willing to bet he was too; he'd had hours to talk to them. The dear Lord only knew what they'd told him!

Thrusting back the covers, she swung her legs from the bed, tugging at the jersey which had ridden up during the night. Something about the gesture caught her attention, and she sat on the bed in frowning stillness as she tried to remember.

The dream. Purple stars and a magical Indian. Closeness and need and desire. Passion and . . . love.

Bemusedly, she watched every detail of the dream float lazily through her mind. How odd—she'd never before remembered a dream so clearly. She felt her heart begin its jungle-pounding and her skin tingle at the memory of rough hands touching her tenderly, warm velvet lips kissing her with adoring passion.

The breath escaped her in a little sigh as the room came into focus again. For heaven's sake— the man had her so rattled she was even dreaming about him. And what a dream! She only hoped that the sounds she remembered uttering had emerged only in her mind.

What the dream really meant, she didn't want to think about. She wasn't about to analyze the deep impulses that had triggered it.

The phone on the nightstand rang shrilly just

then, and C.J. frowned at it a moment before reaching to pick up the receiver. "Hello?"

"Are you awake?" Jan demanded without preamble.

"Of course I'm awake." C.J. frowned at her reflection in the mirror across the room, not liking the softened, dreamy expression in her eyes.

"There's no 'of course' about it, damnit. I've called you twice since eight o'clock this morning, and you answered the phone both times. But you weren't awake. You've got Fate all shook up; he's not used to these weird sleeps of yours."

"Um . . . he's with you?" C.J.'s voice was a masterpiece of casual unconcern.

"He's been with us all morning. Shame on you, C.J.—you haven't told the poor man a thing about yourself!"

"If you told him—" C.J. began heatedly.

"No, of course we didn't tell him your name," Jan broke in soothingly. "But you'll have to tell him sometime, sweetie, for the marriage license if nothing else." She laughed suddenly. "I must admit that listening to him try to charm the name out of us was some experience! That's quite a man you have there."

"Yes," C.J. murmured in a flattened voice. "Quite a man. He—uh—he asked you about me?"

"All about you. From the cradle onward. And we told him everything we knew. Under the circumstances, we didn't think you'd mind." There was something half triumphant and half questioning in Jan's voice.

"No. I don't mind . . . at all." C.J. wondered vaguely if Fate was, in fact, an Indian. If so, she couldn't understand how the Indians had managed finally to lose the war.

"I was a little suspicious last night," Jan went on cheerfully, "but after he spent the night in your room, I realized that the whole thing was on the level."

Score one for Fate! C.J. thought, amused in spite of herself. He'd neatly pegged Jan.

"You've got some explaining to do, my girl!"

"Didn't Fate explain?" C.J. asked hopefully, reasonably certain that he had, but half afraid of what he might have come up with.

"Why you didn't tell us? He said it was probably because you weren't quite sure what was going on yourself. Everything happened so fast, and he couldn't tell you what was wrong. Was that it?"

"Yes," C.J. murmured with a faint sigh, "that was it." She was relieved that Fate had answered that question. It was going to be hard enough to play her role of a woman in love without having to elaborate on his absurd story.

"You still should have told us," Jan scolded gently. "It can't have been easy for you, C.J. In love for the first time and not knowing why you couldn't be together. We could have helped."

"I know. And I'm sorry. I was just so confused." C.J. felt like the worst kind of liar. *Damn* her stupid impulses, and damn Fate for throwing himself wholeheartedly into the charade!

"Well, at least it's over now. And you'll be walking down the aisle next month. I never thought I'd be saying that, sweetie!"

Hastily, C.J. said, "Let's not talk about that now. This is Kathy's time, remember? We have to get through her wedding first."

"We could make it a double wedding," Jan pointed out suggestively.

"No!" C.J. knew that her voice was too sharp, and rushed on before Jan could notice it. "Like you said, Fate doesn't know too much about me. And I don't know much about him. We need a little time, Jan."

Jan sighed. "You're right, of course. But it would have been perfect. Oh, well." The mouthpiece was muffled as she apparently spoke to someone nearby, and then she came back on the line. "When are you coming down? We want to have lunch and then hit the slopes."

"Fifteen minutes," C.J. managed lightly.

"Great. See you in the lobby."

C.J. replaced the received slowly and stared at the phone for a long moment. So Fate had worked his way into the magic circle. He had charmed her friends, and spent the morning asking them all about her.

That put him one up on her; she still knew nothing about him.

She got up and began getting ready to go downstairs, a frown drawing her brows together. In for the duration, with Fate one step ahead of her. It made her very uneasy.

She was halfway to the door when a sudden thought stopped her in her tracks.

"Don't be ridiculous," she said nervously to the empty room. "It was a dream. Wasn't it?"

Four

Forever afterward, C.J. maintained that that day was among the worst in her life. Pitchforked into a role she had absolutely no idea how to play, she cringed inwardly beneath the watching eyes of her friends and silently cursed Fate in every language she knew and a few she made up.

And he took advantage of the situation, the fiend. When the girls showed rare tact and offered to leave them alone together, Fate wouldn't hear of it. He organized ridiculous games on skis, keeping them together and laughing; he issued challenges the girls couldn't resist; and he managed adroitly to keep C.J. with or near him at all times.

He hugged her, held her hand (even on skis), sprinkled his conversation with endless endearments. He teased her in what C.J. imagined must be a loverlike manner. He kept trying to discover her name, and seemed crestfallen when his guesses were wrong.

"Cheryl Jane?"

"No." C.J. firmly pried her hand from his and

used her poles to push off down the slope. It was an advanced slope, and she hoped that it would discourage both Fate and the girls from staying too close to her. But they were all expert on skis, and Fate was Olympic-team material.

They didn't leave her alone for a minute.

It went on that way for the rest of the day and into the evening. C.J. kept a smile plastered on her face and looked daggers at Fate whenever she was reasonably certain the girls wouldn't see. Not that it made the slightest impression on him.

She left dinner early pleading a headache, and gritted her teeth as she saw Fate wink at the girls before rising himself. He kept a loverlike arm around her until they were in the elevator and C.J. shrugged it away.

She stared stonily at the doors as they rode upward, aware that he was leaning against the wall with his arms folded and his eyes fixed on her. She didn't return the steady, smiling gaze. She was torn between screaming at him in frustrated rage—an unfamiliar emotion—and throwing herself wantonly into his arms, compelled by an altogether different emotion.

She felt like a see-saw, a yo-yo. Up and down, back and forth, tormented by crazy impulses she'd never felt before. And it was all his fault, damnit. Even telling herself that the day's cherishing touches and teasing words were just a part of his charade, she'd been fighting her instinct to respond to them all day.

"You look like a sulky little girl," he said as the doors opened and they left the elevator on their floor.

Not rising to the bait, she said tautly, "And you're definitely a long-legged beastie."

"I'm a what?" He halted beside her as they

reached the door to her room and she fished in the pocket of her slacks for her key.

"Haven't you ever heard that old Scottish prayer?" Refusing to look at him, C.J. unlocked the door. " 'From ghoulies and ghosties and long-legged beasties and things that go bump in the night— Good Lord deliver us.' "

"I take it that wasn't a compliment." He sounded amused, grasping her arm when she would have entered the room.

"Bingo." She stared fixedly at some point near the middle of his chest. "Charade's over for the night. I'm going to soak in the tub and read a good book; you're on your own. The girls will never know you aren't in my room. Goodnight." She heard the elevator bell ding softly.

"Too late," he murmured. "They're coming now." Before she could utter a protest or sound, he drew her swiftly into his arms.

She looked up, filled with unreasoning panic, just as his lips covered hers. In those first few moments, she struggled inwardly against shrieking nerve endings and disordered thoughts, her body remaining stiff in his arms. Her mouth was closed desperately to resist his invasion, and she fiercely called upon the concentration she'd taught herself so many years ago.

But her concentration had never run head-on into Fate.

His lips played on hers with the delicate touch of a master, soft and pleading for a response. She felt the tip of his tongue probing gently, insistently. Strong arms pulled her even closer, one of his hands sliding down her back to her hips, pressing her against the lean strength of his body until she could feel the throbbing desire he made no effort to hide.

An ache began in the pit of her belly, startling

her with its suddenness. She felt her arms sliding around his waist, her lips parting with a will of their own, and realized in dismay that she had little control over the need he aroused in her.

And then Fate suddenly released her. Blinking dazedly, C.J. saw two total strangers pass them with politely averted eyes. Slowly she understood that he had lied about the girls coming.

Leaning against the doorjamb and all too aware of the unsteady legs supporting her, she stared at him. He appeared perfectly calm. Hands in the pockets of his slacks, he returned her stare with a slight smile. The purple eyes were glowing.

"Goodnight, pixie."

Had she imagined the slight hoarseness in his voice? C.J. took a deep breath and straightened to her full height of barely five feet. "If I were you," she said evenly, "I'd guard my back. Someone's liable to do you a mischief."

"I'll keep that in mind," he responded gravely.

C.J. turned, went into her room, and closed the door behind her with unnatural care. She stood perfectly still for long minutes, until she was sure that he had gone. Then she made a peculiar little sound rather like the snarl of an enraged, frustrated kitten.

Monday and Tuesday were two more candidates for C.J.'s list of one lifetime's very worst days. Fate continued to ingratiate himself with the girls and smother her with loving attention. He pulled out all the stops in his act of devotion, and it was driving C.J. to the brink of insanity.

And he left her at her door each of the nights with a kiss that kept her awake, alone in her bed, long into the morning hours.

On Wednesday, she was finally granted an opportunity to be alone. Fate excused himself after lunch, pleading important phone calls and leaving C.J. with a passionate kiss which should have branded her for life. She was staring after him dazedly when Jan reminded her that they had planned to go into Aspen to pick up a few last-minute things for the wedding.

Ruthlessly pulling herself together, C.J. said, "I think I'll stay here. See you later."

Tami gave her an arch look. "You're just hoping Fate's phone calls won't take long!"

"I don't blame her." Ann sighed softly. "He's such a sweet man, C.J. Anybody can see he absolutely adores you!"

C.J. managed a weak smile. "See you later," she repeated. *Sweet?* she marveled silently. The man was about as sweet as a cruising shark! Not that her friends could see that; Fate had them thoroughly charmed. All they saw was a man head-over-heels in love with their friend. He was handsome and utterly masculine but not the least bit afraid to be gentle or silly, not the slightest bit self-conscious while uttering loving words. . . .

She found herself thinking about him as she rode the elevator alone up to her room. In fact, he had never been totally out of her thoughts since the moment she'd met him. And that was scary.

She fought the knowledge that the man had charmed her as well as her friends, but lost the fight. He *had* charmed her. She had experienced more emotional ups and downs in the past three days than in her entire life, but there had been moments of sheer absurdity. And, to her surprise, she had discovered within herself a love of the absurd.

Fate made her angry, frustrated her, set her senses in a bewildering spin, shamelessly took advantage of the situation she had created. And he made her laugh. She had to stay on her toes with him; very little got past him.

And there was, she admitted to herself, a certain delight in that. Until now, she'd had very little experience in the art of verbal fencing. But now . . .

The sparring had taken place quite often in the last three days. Sweetly barbed words from her, smiling responses from him. Usually murmured in undertones, since her friends were nearby. Double-edged comments, ironic asides, *sotto voce* remarks.

C.J. thought with surprise that she had never felt so alive, so aware of everything around her. It was another scary thought; a change in her that Fate was responsible for. Fiercely, she pushed him into a corner of her mind and slammed the door on him.

She remained in her room only long enough to find a heavy book in her bag, then headed downstairs again. Due to happy skiers on the slopes on this sunny afternoon, the lounge was deserted.

At last—alone!

C.J. propped her feet on a hassock, smiled happily at the roaring fire in the huge stone fireplace, and opened her book. With a little luck, her friends would be gone for hours, and she could lose herself in history.

Time passed without notice as she absorbed the flavor and color of medieval England. The author of the book was a master storyteller, and dry facts leaped off the page vibrant with life.

She was only dimly aware of shadows passing around her from time to time. Voices bounced off her consciousness without making any noticeable dent. But then one voice began to irritate like a buzzing insect, annoy like a song one couldn't forget.

"C.J.?"

She tuned it out.

"Hey, lady!"

She frowned and concentrated harder.

"Earth calling Miss Adams!"

She flounced around and away from the voice.

"I hate to disturb you, but the couch is on fire."

The laughing male voice finally had the desired effect. With an exasperated sigh, C.J. slammed the book shut. Her glaring yellow eyes slowly traveled up the jean-and-sweater-clad length of a masculine body, settling at last on a solemn Indian face. "Did you want something?" she asked with awful politeness.

"Funny you should ask."

She glanced at the broad watch on her slender wrist and then back up at Fate. "Look, I've only got another hour at most. Will you—"

"Another hour for what?" he interrupted.

"For enjoying myself before the girls come back, whereupon I will become the center of the all-time favorite indoor sport."

"Which is?" His lips twitched.

She smiled very sweetly. "Watching C.J. make a total ass of herself."

Fate laughed and sank down beside her on the couch. "Is that what you've been doing? I hadn't noticed."

"You should have. 'It takes one to know one.' "

"Cruel. You're a cruel lady." He reached over to pluck the book from her hands. "What were you so engrossed in?"

With a certain perverse pleasure, she watched his eyebrows shoot upward and a bemused expression cross his face as he read the book's title aloud.

"*A Study of Medieval Times.*"

"One of my favorites," she told him limpidly.

There was an odd gleam in Fate's dark eyes as he looked up from the book to meet her gaze.

"What did you think of Miller's *Guide to the Medieval Age*?" he asked casually.

"I . . . it was . . . fascinating." C.J. couldn't have been more surprised if he'd suddenly started talking to her in Middle English. Other than actual students of medieval history—precious few of them—she'd never met a man interested in the subject. "You . . . *like* medieval history?"

"All kinds of history." He sat back, carelessly throwing his arm across the back of the couch. "As a kid, I wanted to grow up to be King Arthur; the interest grew out of that. Every elective I could work in during college was on the subject. I couldn't decide whether to become a lawyer or a history teacher."

"But law won." C.J. was burningly aware of the long fingers resting casually on her shoulder.

"In the end. I come from a long line of lawyers, and I wanted to help people in trouble." He shrugged, smiling wryly. "Idealistic maybe, but what the hell. I haven't regretted it."

"Tell me about it." She smiled at his quizzical look. "I want to know—really. Your cases, clients."

"The degenerates," he said teasingly.

C.J. had the grace to blush. "Sorry about that. I was mad."

"I know you were. I seem to have the knack of enraging you, pixie. You spit like a kitten at me."

Not certain that she liked the comparison, C.J. frowned at him. "You were going to tell me about your work," she prompted.

"Was I?" His fingers began playing with the curls around her ear. "I can't imagine why. It's dull, most of it. Boring research and trying to convince reluctant witnesses to testify and arguing precedents in courtrooms."

"No Perry Mason dramatics?" she asked with mock disappointment.

His lips twitched. "So far, no. And no cases needing the genius of Sherlock Holmes to unravel. Just steady, plodding work." He turned his gaze to the fire and the mockery fell away from him as he frowned slightly. "Although there was one case . . ."

C.J. listened, fascinated, as he told her of a man on trial for his life. A murder trial. Fate had spent months sifting through facts and statements from witnesses, prowling the area where the crime had taken place. Convinced of the innocence of his client.

He downplayed his own intelligence in discovering the real murderer, but C.J. wasn't deceived. The real murderer had been totally unsuspected, and she knew that Fate's task had been more than difficult. But a certain amount of courtroom dramatics and a novel-like last-minute revelation of uncovered evidence had cleared his client and pinpointed the real killer.

Asking intelligent questions, C.J. heard more about Fate's cases during past years, and then they wound up talking about history. They discussed C.J.'s topic for her doctoral thesis, exchanged favorite little-known historical facts, argued over which ruler had done the most for his country and civilization as a whole.

It was like pulling teeth, but she even managed to get Fate to talk a little about his background. His family was "average," he said. His younger brother was in college, his parents lived in Wyoming. His father was a retired lawyer, and his mother, also retired, a commercial artist.

They compared childhoods briefly, and talked about schoolday pranks and teenage miseries. Colleges were discussed, and how boring a job could sometimes be, and how irritating it was to have to cook for just one person.

They were no longer—could no longer be—two actors on a stage.

That fact didn't hit C.J. until the next day. High winds made the slopes both uncomfortable and unsafe, with the result that most of the lodge's guests remained inside. The place was by no means too crowded, but one had to take care not to bump into someone while moving through the halls or lounges.

C.J. and her friends were busy getting ready for the wedding on Saturday—to be held in the lodge's lovely chapel—and Fate made himself amazingly useful. Kathy had invited him, days before, to be a part of the ceremony. So he would be ushering C.J. down the aisle a bit early—she a bridesmaid and he an usher.

It was Fate who suggested to Kathy that the entire lodge be invited to participate in the event, pointing out that everyone loved weddings and, besides, the guests would probably welcome a change in their routine. To C.J.'s surprise, Kathy approved of the idea wholeheartedly, and immediately posted a notice on the bulletin board in the lobby.

That instant acceptance of Fate's idea caused C.J. to step back and take a new look at her friends. They all liked Fate. No—more than liked him. They loved him like a brother. In a few short days, he had won them over completely.

C.J. tried to think of him as simply an actor, playing out a role, but the serious man she had talked to the day before kept intruding. From the very beginning, she'd seen him as an attractive man, but the role he played had prevented her from seeing the man himself very clearly. Now she saw the man rather than the actor.

She was still fighting the attraction she felt for him, but she was no longer able to tell herself firmly that she wasn't about to get involved with an obvious lunatic. The man who had talked to her about law and history had been a highly intelligent, perfectly sane man. The fact that the man clearly relished his role as a lover was, therefore, a puzzling mystery.

The only explanation C.J. could come up with was his own: lawyers were apparently frustrated actors at heart.

That oddly angering thought was in her mind on Thursday afternoon when Fate stepped from the elevator just as she was getting ready to enter it. Her arms were full of flowers—silk flowers— which she was going to take to the chapel on the top floor of the lodge. Fate paid absolutely no attention to the colorful burden as he caught her in an abrupt, bone-crushing hug, swinging her around and off her feet.

The elevator doors hissed softly closed as C.J. emerged from the bear hug more than a little breathless. "What was that for?" she asked dazedly. "You win a lottery or something?"

"Every human being," he began, tapping her nose with his index finger to emphasize each word, "needs a minimum of three hugs per day. To ensure mental health."

C.J. blinked with each tap. "Oh, yes? Do you dabble in psychology as well as law and history?"

"I don't dabble in anything," he corrected austerely. "History is a hobby. And every good lawyer studies psychology."

"Every good lawyer shoots bull, too."

"I've never shot a bull in my life."

"Cute, Maestro. That's cute. All you need is a stage and footlights to be right in your element."

"Uh oh." He slid his hands into his pockets and

rocked back on his heels, head held to one side consideringly. "She's mad at me again," he announced, as though to a third person. "After twenty-four glorious hours of not being mad at me, I've done something to set her off again. Whatever could I have done?"

"Just being you is enough," she said sweetly.

"Ouch." He looked wounded.

"You're making fools out of my friends—and me!" she accused, feeling herself building toward a full head of steam. That her anger was irrational in a situation she'd brought on herself, she didn't consider. It was enough that the emotional upsets of the past days had taken their toll, and she wanted somebody to suffer the consequences. And since it was his fault, he could suffer.

"I did that?" he queried innocently.

"You know exactly what you've been doing! My friends think the sun rises and sets on you. They don't know you're an utterly unscrupulous, conniving, deceitful—"

"Into the trenches and guard your back, man," he warned himself lightly. "She's about to commence a pitched battle!"

"Stop laughing at me!" C.J. all but stamped her foot. "You should get an Oscar for this performance, d'you know that? You play the part of lover better than Romeo did! And I'm fed up with—"

"So *that's* it!" he exclaimed softly, a spark of something very like satisfaction glowing in the purple eyes.

"So *what's* it?" she demanded irritably.

"You're mad because I've played my part too well. The courtship's really beginning to get to you, isn't it, pixie?"

"Don't flatter yourself!" she snapped.

"Admit it—you're beginning to believe that a passionate love affair wouldn't be such a bad idea after all. I've got you so confused, you don't know what you want."

This time, C.J. did stamp her foot. "Quit twisting things around!" she snarled. "This whole idea was a bad one from start to finish, and you know it as well as I do!" She felt tears of frustration rise in her eyes, and was astonished by this display of weakness.

"Poor baby." Fate was abruptly grave, remorse showing on his face and in his eyes. "I really have got you upset. Would it help to apologize on bended knees?"

"No," she muttered, uncertain whether or not the remorse was real, but suspicious.

"How about if I apologize à la Valentino?" Without giving her a chance to respond, he suddenly caught her around the waist with one arm, bending her back until he was supporting most of her weight and she was very nearly horizontal from the waist up.

Blinking up at him and clutching his sweater instinctively, C.J. stared up at dark eyes dramatically narrowed to veil an imaginary desert sun, and choked back an irrepressible giggle. The sudden absurdity had drained away her anger, and she almost hated him for that. "You've been watching too many old movies."

"Forgive me, my darling," he pleaded in a heavily accented voice, splendidly ignoring her unromantic comment. "I would cut my throat before harming you, my treasure!"

Before C.J. could respond—fortunately—a laughing female voice intruded.

"Is this an X-rated movie, or can I watch?" Jan asked wryly.

C.J. found herself watching his profile as Fate turned his head to speak to her friend, feeling absolutely ridiculous dangling over his arm like a coat.

"I'm apologizing to C.J.," Fate told Jan politely.

"Must have been some fight," she observed. "Whatever did you do?"

"I'm not sure, but she was upset."

"It takes an utter fiend to rouse C.J."

"I'm crushed. What can I do to make it up to her?"

"Shower her with flowers and chocolates."

"She's got flowers," he pointed out reasonably.

"You've crushed them. And they were for the chapel, anyway."

"Were they? I wondered. Should I buy her some real ones?"

"Yes. And chocolates."

"Why chocolates?"

"She loves them."

Still dangling, C.J. conjured a mental image of what she must look like. A still clip from one of Valentino's movies came to mind. "Hello," she murmured. "Remember me?"

Fate turned his head to stare down at her. "Hello," he said in mock surprise. "What are you doing there?"

C.J. swallowed a giggle. "Beats the hell out of me."

"You've taught her to swear." Jan brushed past them to enter the elevator as the doors slid open to discharge three people. "Wonderful. I didn't think she'd ever get the hang of it. Bye, now."

Feeling herself turning red, C.J. watched the three people, who averted their eyes politely but didn't bother to hide their grinning mouths. When they had disappeared from view, she returned her gaze to Fate's face. "Is the show over?" she asked with infinite patience.

"Not until you forgive me."

"For what?" C.J. had somehow lost sight of the original point of all this.

"For upsetting you. Am I forgiven?"

"I suppose. Will you let me go now?"

"That wasn't a very gracious acceptance of my apology," he pointed out critically. "Try again."

"I forgive you. *Now* will you let me go?"

"Now promise not to get mad at me again."

"I'm getting a crick in my back," she evaded.

"Promise."

C.J. wished suddenly that she had long fingernails so that she could dig them into his chest. "I never make promises I can't keep."

"Then promise you'll *try* not to get mad at me."

"And deprive myself of my only pleasure? No way. Will you please let me go before I'm convinced you're more depraved than I originally thought you were?"

Fate sighed and allowed her to straighten, dropping his arm when she was in balance again. "As I believe I've remarked once before, you're a cruel lady. I don't ask for much, after all—"

"Of course not," she interrupted ironically, giving the crushed flowers in her arms a disgusted look. "Just look what you've done! They're ruined."

"Sorry about that." He didn't sound it.

"I'll bet. You're a menace, Maestro, an absolute menace."

"I aim to please," he disclaimed modestly.

"Can't you be serious just for a minute?"

"Oh, but I am." He smiled slowly. "I've been serious all along, pixie. You just haven't realized it yet."

For no reason she could understand, C.J. felt a curious tension steal through her body. She clutched the ruined flowers to her breast and stared at him warily, at a loss to understand or interpret the expression in his eyes. Waiting? No, not exactly. Anxious? No—ridiculous. Why was he looking at her like that?

Fate reached out suddenly and ran a finger lightly down her cheek. "Not ready yet, huh?"

"Ready for what?" she asked uneasily, unconsciously crushing the flowers a bit more.

He grinned, laughter gleaming in the dark eyes. "You are a constant delight to me, do you know that? I can always count on you to take the wind out of my sails!" He laughed at some private joke, then leaned over and kissed her swiftly. "See you later."

Perplexed, C.J. stared after him until he had disappeared from her sight. "If I live to be a hundred," she told the empty lobby vaguely, "I will never figure that man out." Shaking her head in bemusement, she went to replace the crushed flowers.

Fate ran her down in one of the lounges later that afternoon. She was sitting before the fire and resting her feet, which were aching from running errands all afternoon.

"There you are!" He thrust heavy mug into her hands and sat down beside her on the couch, throwing a careless arm over the back of the couch behind her. "I've been looking everywhere."

C.J. peered into the dark brown liquid that filled her mug and the identical mug in his hand. "What's this?"

"Cocoa. The gift shop's closed, and this was the only kind of chocolate I could find."

"Thank you," she said, hiding a smile as she sipped the drink and remembered Jan's earlier advice to him. After a moment, she went on meditatively, "Do you know that there's a chemical in cocoa which is also a chemical that is released by the brain when one falls in love? I suppose that's why chocolates have always been considered a meaningful courtship gift."

His eyes lit with amusement. "Are you suggesting—?"

"Well, why not? It'd explain—at least in part—the divorce rate. Candy consumed, chemical vanishes . . . and suddenly love isn't quite as strong as one thought it was."

"That's a cynical thought."

"Isn't it?"

"Don't you believe in love?"

"Oh, sure." She stared fixedly into her cocoa. "But I think it's a very misused word. People say love when they really mean any number of other things."

"And can you define real love?" he challenged smoothly.

C.J. lifted her eyes to stare into the fire, and seriously considered his question. "Real love . . . is sharing," she said finally. "Sharing dreams, and laughter, and things that are important to you. Sharing bad times as well as good ones. It's . . . a closeness. A feeling that the one you love . . . sees you in a way no one else does. Knows you better than you know yourself . . ." Her voice trailed away.

The hand behind her dropped to grasp her shoulder as Fate gave her a sudden, almost fierce hug. "That's exactly what I think it is," he told her huskily.

C.J. looked at him in surprise, having almost forgotten that he was there. And she had the odd sensation of seeing him for the first time. Gazing beyond the facade of his role, past the layer of the intelligent attorney, beneath the charming, little-boy mischief. And what she saw kept her completely motionless as he set his mug on the coffee table and then gently took hers away from her.

A very calm little voice inside her head warned that she should make some movement or utter words to break the sudden, almost painful tension between them. The voice went unheeded.

Fate slid one arm beneath her knees, the other around her back as he lifted her easily into his lap. He took no notice of her soft gasp, holding her eyes with his own. When she was half lying across his lap, her arms moving instinctively to encircle his neck, he whispered roughly, "I won't call it love, because you wouldn't believe me, but I want you, pixie."

C.J. felt herself getting lost somewhere in the purple depths of his eyes, until his lips touched hers, her long lashes fluttered down, and another, deeper, sigh escaped her.

There was no gentle plea in this kiss, no appeal for a response. His lips plundered her own with a demand which stopped just short of violence. He was taking as though he had a right to.

She granted him the right that he took. Shaken by the wild need surging through her body, there was nothing else she could do. It no longer seemed to matter that his motives were unclear or that she didn't understand him. She accepted his words at face value. He wanted her.

And she silently acknowledged for the first time that she wanted him as well. Desire and need ate at her, filling her body with an empty ache only he could assuage.

The admission made, C.J. no longer made any effort to hold back or deny her response to him. Her fingers twined among the soft strands of his dark hair, her body twisted in an effort to be closer to him. She felt her breasts crushed against his muscled chest and, even through the bulky barriers of two sweaters, was aware of her nipples hardening in aching response.

Rough hands slipped beneath her sweater to touch the smooth skin of her back, drawing her closer, trailing fire wherever they paused. His lips slanted across hers with driving hunger, seducing her, teaching her to respond only to his touch.

And respond she did, her mouth clinging to his, her tongue joining his in a passionate, desperate duel as old as the stars. For her, the world vanished. There was only this flaming desire, this hurting need to be closer to him than she could possibly be, to become a part of him.

"Lord, you're so sweet," he muttered hoarsely when his mouth left hers at last to burn the sensitive flesh of her throat. "So warm and sweet, darling . . ."

C.J. only dimly heard his words, her head tilted back to allow his exploring lips to ravage where they would. She was floating somewhere magical, bewitched and enchanted.

The fall back to earth, when it came, was abrupt and complete. And C.J. didn't know whether to scream in frustration or to laugh in hysterical relief.

"Hey, lovebirds—we're going to get ready for dinner. Are you interested? Or should I bite my tongue?"

It was Jan, standing with the other girls in the doorway to the lounge, and smiling wickedly at the couple alone in the room. Several giggles and one "Whew!" followed her words.

C.J. stared into glazed purple eyes for a timeless moment, and then scrambled hurriedly from Fate's lap. Too stunned by her own response to be embarrassed, she smoothed her sweater into place and murmured, "Dinner. Of course."

'In just the same way she would have said—"Thank goodness, saved by the bell."

Five

The talk around their table later that evening was casual, centered mainly around the following night's party, which the management at the lodge had decided to throw. It was their contribution to the festive mood that had gripped the guests all day, a warm-up—so to speak—for Saturday's wedding. Semiformal, it had been decided, with everyone doing the best they could in the way of clothing.

C.J.'s friends being what they were, there was no lack of formal dress within the group. In addition to their bridesmaid dresses, each had brought along dressy things "just in case." Like Boy Scouts, they believed in being prepared.

Except, of course, for C.J. Even Fate admitted that he'd brought a dinner jacket along.

Listening to the others talking, C.J. kept her eyes lowered to her plate. She wasn't thinking about what had happened in the lounge earlier; thinking about that, she had discovered, was somewhat like considering a dip in a pool filled with hungry sharks. Scary.

She was waiting for her friends to start in on her. They knew very well that she hadn't brought along anything except her bridesmaid dress. However, for quite some time nothing was said about her lack of preparedness. The girls were excited because their husbands were arriving the next day, and were busy giving Fate thumbnail sketches of each man.

Actually, it wasn't until several hours later when they were all sitting around the fire in one of the lounges that the attack commenced. C.J. was trying to ignore the fact that Fate, close beside her, was holding her hand and playing with her fingers, so she was caught off guard when the subject finally came up.

"Oh, no!" Kathy groaned suddenly. "What are we going to do about C.J.?"

Fate looked surprised, but five pairs of eyes turned to C.J. with varying degrees of exasperation. She blinked at them, and wondered absently if Fate had noticed that her hands were cold.

"Trade her in for a new model," Jan suggested wryly.

Kathy sighed. "I have a dress she can wear," she volunteered. "It'll be a little tight across the bust—damnit—but I doubt that anyone'll mind."

"I certainly won't mind," Fate inserted cheerfully.

"You wouldn't!" Tami laughed.

"Ann, did you bring your curlers? We can roll her hair in the morning—"

"Her hands are hopeless! She *will* keep her nails short in spite of everything I tell her—"

"Shoes! Kathy, your feet are nearly as small as hers. Did you bring that pair of black pumps along—?"

"At least her ears are pierced. I have those pearl studs that my grandmother gave me—"

"I bet the holes have closed up; I haven't seen

her wear earrings since my wedding, and *that* was September—"

"I have a silk shawl she can borrow."

C.J. listened mutely to these plans for her transformation. But now, unlike all the times in the past, she got mad. She wasn't sure exactly why, and didn't stop to question it. She just knew that she was fed up with being dictated to as though she were a child.

She said nothing, however, very much aware of Fate at her side. He was throwing in a comment now and then, teasing C.J. right along with the rest of them. He seemed to think the whole thing highly amusing, and played it for all it was worth.

At the end of half an hour, C.J.'s mad was simmering and she was beginning to feel sorry for herself. Fate might at least defend her, she thought miserably. He was supposed to be in love with her, for Pete's sake! He was as bad as the rest of them.

She neither agreed nor disagreed with the plans flying round her head, but merely listened with outward meekness. When her friends had finally wound down, she pried her fingers from Fate's and quietly excused herself, pleading tiredness. Fate followed her from the room.

It wasn't until they had nearly reached C.J.'s door that he spoke. "Did it bother you—what your friends were saying?"

"Why should it bother me? They've been saying the same things for years." She got her key out and unlocked the door, refusing to look at him until he grasped her arm and turned her to face him.

"That's no answer." He stood looking down at her for a long moment, then grinned suddenly. "Tell you what. I'll take you into Aspen tomorrow, and we'll find something really special. Something to startle the hell out of all of them."

She lifted an eyebrow questioningly. "Something—?"

"Something"—he made a curiously graphic gesture with both hands—"slinky."

C.J.'s mad hit boiling point about then, but the lid didn't blow. Not then. "Slinky," she repeated, not sure exactly why she was so utterly furious. "*Slinky.*"

"Sexy," he elaborated—not that he needed to. "I'll bet you're a real knockout when you're all dressed up. What do you say? Will you go into Aspen with me?"

"I'll think about it." She nipped into her room quickly, before he could bestow the usual soul-destroying kiss. "Goodnight." She barely waited for his "Goodnight, pixie" before shutting the door.

Automatically fastening the night chain, C.J. went to get ready for bed. She undressed and then donned the football jersey, washed her face, brushed her teeth, climbed into bed, turned out the light—all without uttering a sound. Then she lay in the wide bed and stared into the darkness.

"Slinky," she muttered. And then, a little louder, "Slinky!" And finally, in a voice that hit about seven on the Richter scale, "*Slinky!*"

C.J. crept out of the lodge at the crack of dawn the next morning, after leaving a vague message for anyone who asked at the desk. She had both her charge cards and her checkbook, and roughly four hours of sleep had done absolutely nothing to diminish her anger.

The cab deposited her in the heart of Aspen. She found a restaurant serving breakfast and ordered more than usual because she had a feeling she was going to need the energy. Then she asked for a phone and a directory. Receiving both, she let her fingers do the walking for a while, then made several local calls and one long-distance one to her banker in Boston. She got him out of bed, but since her business account was one of the largest in the bank, he didn't protest after he realized who was calling.

The conversation was short on C.J.'s part, confined to a single request which her banker readily agreed to without surprise or undue curiosity. Since his business dealings with Miss Adams had shown her to be a level-headed, shrewd woman, he neither treated her like a child nor demanded to know what she was up to. And he would be quite happy to call the bank in Aspen and okay a substantial withdrawal.

That done, C.J. sat for a moment and chewed on her thumb thoughtfully. Jewelry. She had little jewelry at home, but that in no way implied ignorance of the subject. In fact, she was very nearly an expert in the fine art of judging fine jewelry; her Uncle John had been a connoisseur, and had taught her all he knew. So she needed no advice with that.

Her breakfast arrived, and C.J. absently began eating.

The salon would be ready for her at three this afternoon. As soon as the bank opened, she'd trot over there. Then the boutiques.

And so she planned, with feminine instincts older than man. . . .

Various shopkeepers, quite a few onlookers, and one cab driver were treated to a very interesting day. The petite redhead dived into and out of stores with bewildering energy, pointing out what she wanted without hesitation and not arguing over prices. Boxes piled up in the back of the cab, and the driver, glancing at his ticking meter, had no doubt that the lady could afford him.

Not for nothing had C.J. watched her friends for twenty years! She was a little startled at the amount that had sunk in over this time, unaware that her feminine instincts were finally coming to the fore. She knew only that she was very weary of being the butt of her friends' jokes.

Several people were startled and puzzled by the remarks left floating in the air as they passed a redhead with glittering yellow eyes.

"Slinky! . . . I'll show them. . . . Think I'm so stupid I don't even know how to wear panty hose, for heaven's sake . . . And *him*, the arrogant, cocksure . . . I'll startle the hell out of them, all right. . . . *Slinky! . . .*"

After a brief halt for lunch, C.J. finally found what she'd been searching for all day. She immediately went into the small, expensive boutique after seeing the dress in the window. Moments later, she was standing in front of a full-length mirror and staring with surprise at her reflection.

"Wicked!" the saleslady exclaimed under her breath. "Miss Adams, I've never seen anything so . . . That dress was made for you!" And her comments were not entirely due to the huge commission she stood to make.

C.J. stared into the mirror for a long time, turning slowly this way and that. Uneasy for the first time, she murmured, "I won't be able to wear anything under it."

"You don't need to," the saleslady said enviously. "But if it bothers you—being so revealing, I mean— there's a lace jacket that would go perfectly—"

"Oh, no!" C.J. interrupted decisively. "I want it revealing. I want it so revealing that I just . . . might . . . get arrested."

"You just might," the older woman murmured. "In fact—you'd cause a pile-up at any intersection in the world!"

C.J. turned to her with an unconsciously feline smile. "I'll take it."

Hours later she sat back on her bed and stared at the boxes piled all around her. She had managed to creep into the lodge unseen by either Fate or her friends—even though it had taken two bellmen to carry the packages.

She opened one of the jeweler's boxes and thoughtfully exchanged her broad, masculine watch for the delicate one in the box. Perfect. It even made her hands look smaller and more . . . feminine. And the manicure had helped there. So would the diamond cluster she had unexpectedly fallen in love with.

Thoughtfully, C.J. began to unpack the boxes and put things away. She was more than a little astonished to realize that she'd spent more money on herself today than she had in years. And it slowly came to her that it hadn't been because of temper alone.

So the butterfly had truly emerged. And this time it wasn't a stranger's face in the mirror. This time it was her.

There were some things, she was ruefully aware, which would never change. She'd always lose herself in history. And she'd always be more apt to wear jeans than a dress. But she would no longer view the world through a gauzy curtain of abstraction, uninterested in joining the parade. Observing the parade had been interesting . . . but marching along with it was fascinating.

Intuitively she understood that marching along with the parade would give her more than blisters on her heels. Already she was feeling the emotional uncertainty of her first relationship with a man . . . be it a farcical relationship, and be he an actor on a stage of her making.

That damned lawyer/actor/Indian had somehow managed to worm his way under her skin.

C.J. accepted this as fact, but she made no attempt to pursue the matter any further. Things like that generally left one feeling like a dog after a fruitless hour of chasing its tail. Nothing very much was accomplished . . . and one got so *tired.*

Instead she began to get ready for the party. In the shower, she reflected that everyone was probably furious with her. She hadn't been here to meet the guys who—the desk clerk had informed her—had arrived safely around lunchtime. She hadn't been very specific in her message about where she was going or what she planned to do, and she had been gone all day.

Oh, well.

The phone rang just as she came out, wrapped in a towel. She pushed several empty boxes out of the way in order to sit on the bed as she lifted the receiver.

"Hello?"

"Where," Fate asked with obvious restraint, "have you been all day?"

"Out." C.J. carefully inspected her polished fingernails.

There were several moments of silence, and then his voice—still carefully polite—went on. "I don't suppose it occurred to you that anyone would worry?"

"I left a message," she pointed out in a voice calculated to drive a saint to murder.

There was another silence. "Great. Unfortunately, your message didn't tell me how to deal with four suspicious husbands and one—ditto the suspicious—'fiancé.'

"Oh, have you had a rough day?" she asked in a spuriously sympathetic tone.

"Not at all," he disclaimed courteously. "I *like*

having five men—three of whom are bigger than I am—gaze at me as though they'd just discovered me in their sister's bed."

In a considering tone, C.J. corrected, "Keith and John aren't bigger, they're just as tall as you. Patrick is bigger. He plays hockey."

Fate said something that was distinctly unrepeatable.

"Such language," she murmured. "If you used words like that, I'm not surprised they—um—eyed you askance."

"They didn't eye me askance," he said dryly. "They eyed me with utter and complete hostility. I've seen friendlier faces at murder trials. Why didn't you warn me that you had five big brothers?"

"Don't worry." C.J. found that the stranger was in the mirror again, and this time discovered a curious affinity with that very feminine woman. "Tonight I'll prove to them that I'm . . . all grown up."

"C.J.—what have you done?" he asked, a sudden wariness in his voice.

"I've spread my wings," she said, more to the lady in the mirror than to him.

"Is that supposed to make sense?" he demanded. "What have you been doing today?"

"Shopping. Something slinky, you said. Remember?"

There was a long silence. "Maybe I'd better see that 'something slinky' before everyone else does," he suggested.

"Oh, I don't think so." Her voice was calm. "Are we dressing for the party and then having dinner?"

"Yes." He sounded a bit distracted. "We're meeting in the dining room. C.J.—"

"Fine, then I'll see you there. Tell everyone to go ahead and order; I may be late."

"I'll stop by and pick you up. We can go down together."

"No. Meet me in the dining room." She hesitated, then added softly, "Please?" She could have sworn he caught his breath.

"All right, pixie," he said finally, a curious huskiness in his deep voice. "But if you come down wearing a washcloth or something, I'll—"

"It's not a washcloth," she said, gazing thoughtfully at the dress lying across the foot of the bed. "There's a little more to it than that."

"Oh Lord," he muttered forebodingly.

"See you at dinner." She cradled the receiver gently.

C.J. took her time getting ready. She applied makeup carefully, covering her freckles—luckily, they were only on her nose—and emphasizing the slant and color of her eyes. Outlining her lips delicately and filling in a soft rose color.

A brand new bottle of perfume was opened, alluring scent placed carefully, thoughtfully. Hidden, secret places.

Diamond studs were placed in her earlobes. A delicate necklace clasped around her neck, the little heart, shaped in diamonds, lying in the valley between her breasts. A matching bracelet was looped around her right wrist. The jeweled watch on the left. The diamond cluster graced the third finger of her right hand.

Then the dress.

It was stark, unrelieved, unadorned black. It was, as the saleslady had said involuntarily, wicked. Backless to just past the beginning of the outward slope of her bottom. Slit up the front of the skirt almost to the apex of her thighs. Two narrow, delicate straps fastened around her neck and widened only slightly as they came down to cover her full breasts before joining in a plunging vee.

And it clung like a live thing everywhere it touched.

C.J. slipped on the black sandals, remembering her search to find shoes with high heels, yet comfortable enough so that her inexperienced feet would feel safe. She didn't want to make a fool of herself by falling flat on her face!

When she finally looked into the mirror, she stood transfixed for a long moment.

The hairstyle chosen by the salon was deceptively simple. Her copper curls had been swept up off her neck and allowed to cluster on the top of her head and over her forehead, making her look somehow taller and more sophisticated and yet softening her face. The makeup had given her a curiously innocent/sexy look, the catlike eyes mysterious and yet shy. Or maybe that was just her own astonishment at the transformation.

C.J. watched a hand come up as though to guard a suddenly vulnerable throat, and felt butterflies chasing one another through her stomach. Was this really she?

It was . . . a merging, a blending of the girl she had been and the woman who had peeked out of her eyes during unguarded moments.

She bent slowly to pick up the black clutch purse on the bed, her eyes still fixed on the mirror. She located her room key on the dresser by touch alone and dropped it into the bag. Finally tearing her gaze from the mirror, she found a compact, her lipstick, and a handkerchief, and dropped them in, too.

A glance at her watch showed her that the others would most likely be at dinner by now. She couldn't stall any longer. Sighing with a mixture of nervousness and excitement, she left the room.

She met no one in the hall or the elevator, and it wasn't until she was crossing the lobby that her flagging confidence received the boost it needed.

The desk clerk let out a long, low wolf-whistle.

C.J. flashed him a grateful smile and then walked steadily toward the dining room. She was by no means a shy woman, but the thought of entering a crowded room wearing this dress was beginning to drain all the strength from her knees. The whistle helped.

The buzz of conversation reached her before she reached the doorway, and she wanted suddenly to turn and walk—run—back to her room. But she squared her shoulders, took a deep breath, and went in. She hesitated for a moment on the threshold, her eyes searching for Fate and her friends.

She had finally located them near the center, when she suddenly became aware that a silence had spread through the room. She saw a sea of faces turned toward her either unobtrusively or openly, and fought a panicky urge to run. Then she saw Fate rise slowly from his chair, his lean face turned toward her with an expression compounded of surprise and a curious satisfaction.

The silence in the room, though momentary, was complete, and C.J. paused, unnerved by the attention she had drawn. Then conversation resumed and she started toward Fate and her friends. Her first few steps possessed all the grace of a puppet whose strings were being jerked by a novice hand, but then something happened.

As she neared the table, the expression in Fate's eyes touched the woman in her, and her embarrassment and nervousness melted away. That look was warm, caressing, and indescribably male. And she covered those last few steps with all the natural grace of a woman—a beautiful, exciting woman—who was approaching a handsome man.

He caught her hand and lifted it to his lips as she halted before him. "You are beautiful," he breathed huskily, his purple eyes glowing and gazing down at her with open, unabashed admiration.

It had all been worth it, C.J. thought dimly as she smiled up at him with the shy, bewitching smile she had no awareness of. This moment made everything worth it. The lack of sleep, her temper, the exhausting day and her unnerving emotional discoveries—none of it mattered now.

"Thank you," she murmured, shy with him for the first time. She sat down in her chair as he pulled it out for her, feeling a queer, giddy sense of happiness when he didn't release her hand. He sat down beside her, their eyes still locked together, and she thought to herself that he looked even more like an Indian in his black dinner jacket. And almost painfully handsome.

Finally tearing her gaze from his, she looked around at her friends and fought to hide a smile. They looked as though they'd been sand-bagged, she decided. Particularly the guys.

Like the women they were married and/or engaged to, the five men were a varied lot. Brian Rush, Jan's husband, was of medium height and stocky, blond like his wife and quiet by nature. Patrick Lyons, Kathy's fiancé, was tall and powerfully built; the largest man in the group, he was also the most gentle. John Crane, Tami's husband, was tall, thin, and lanky, a redhead with green eyes and a startlingly deep voice. Chris Morgan, Susan's husband, was an inch shorter than his tall wife, dark and gray-eyed, with a quick, friendly smile. And last of all was Keith Butler, Ann's husband. He was tall, slender, always calm, with shrewd blue eyes and auburn hair.

They were all handsome, intelligent men. And all had regarded C.J. as a little sister from the moment of their entrance into the magic circle. They watched over and protected her just as real brothers would have done. And all were now gazing at her with the startled, somewhat embarrassed eyes of men who had suddenly discovered that "little sister" was all grown up.

All except for Keith, that is, who never seemed startled by anything. But he looked thoughtful, the shrewd blue eyes moving from C.J.'s face to Fate's and back again.

Breaking the long silence, C.J. smiled at all of them. "Hi, guys," she said lightly. "Sorry I wasn't here to meet you; I had some things to take care of in Aspen."

"You look lovely, C.J.," Keith said quietly.

C.J. gave him a surprised look, but smiled in acknowledgment of that and the somewhat hastily added compliments from the other men. "Thank you. Have you all ordered yet? I'm starved . . ."

It was a strange meal.

A bubble of laughter remained in the back of C.J.'s throat from the moment she realized that Fate had not exaggerated by saying that the guys were both suspicious and hostile. As soon as the shock of C.J.'s entrance wore off, the hostility—controlled but visible—returned in force.

And that hostility was probably, C.J. thought, stronger than it had been earlier in the day. Because the guys now realized that they were no longer watching over a little girl, but a woman. And a handsome man, they seemed to think, was far more dangerous to a big girl than a little one.

But what tickled C.J. more than anything else was the knowledge that Fate was no longer having everything his own way. Wisely, he didn't try the parasite-and-laser beam story on them, although he must have known that the girls would have already relayed that. So he met hostility with easy friendliness and suspicion with bland in-comprehension. He seemed perfectly calm, but C.J. could feel the tension in him, and wondered with amusement if he were afraid the situation would come to swords-or-pistols-at-dawn.

She wondered if the girls thought so, too. They were unusually quiet, and somewhat anxiously helped Fate in trying to promote a more relaxed atmosphere among the men.

C.J. herself did nothing to ease the tension. She smiled gently at Fate whenever he looked at her, accepted his loving attention with utter calm, and fought to keep from laughing out loud.

As the meal wore on, that task became harder. The guys fired questions at him as though he were in the witness stand—a new experience for him, C.J. felt sure—and seemed dissatisfied with all his answers. Even gentle Patrick was aroused to a glare when Fate declared that he liked foot-ball better than hockey.

Only Keith displayed no fierce protective emotion, but he retired behind a wall of reserve every bit as unbreachable as the open hostility of the others. He did, however, blink when Fate put an arm around C.J. between the final course and dessert.

"You're not helping a bit," Fate muttered into her ear, under the guise of nuzzling her temple.

"Into the trenches and guard your back," she murmured, repeating an earlier phrase of his in reply.

"Thanks!" he whispered irritably.

"Where's that famous charm?" she asked sweetly in a low tone as she leaned back to allow the waiter to place her dessert before her.

"The hell with charm. Do any of these guys know karate?"

"Only Brian," she told him limpidly. "Of course, Patrick's very good with a stick—any kind of stick."

And I think that Keith was with the marines in 'Nam. . . ."

Fate attacked his dessert as though he wished it were something else entirely.

Hiding a smile, C.J. looked away and met Keith's thoughtful gaze. She wondered if he had overheard her soft conversation with Fate, but his veiled eyes gave her no clue. He raised his wine glass slightly in a tiny salute, and she thought that a smile glimmered briefly in his blue eyes before he turned in response to something Ann had said to him.

A little uneasy, C.J. remembered that Keith, like Fate, rarely missed anything. What was he thinking?

After the meal, they joined others making their way to the largest lounge, where the party was to take place. Fate took the opportunity to whisper a few more words of reproach into C.J.'s ear as they moved with the crowd.

"I hope revenge is sweet."

"Very sweet."

"You little witch, you enjoyed that!"

C.J. smiled up at him. "Immensely."

Fate was distracted for a moment, noting that John was glaring pointedly at the hand resting on the small of C.J.'s bare back. Hastily, the hand slid upward a few discreet inches. "Damn! I feel like a white slaver, the way they're looking at me."

"It isn't so much fun when it's an uphill struggle, is it?" she asked him wryly.

He looked down at her. "Are you trying to make a point?"

"I wondered when you'd notice."

Fate sighed. "Touché. But you haven't had to deal with five hostile men."

"No. Just one crazy man."

"I resent that," he said, looking absurdly wounded.

C.J. wasn't deceived. "Sure. If you want some advice—"

"Now she offers!" he interrupted, looking heavenward.

"—you'll tone down the loving act," she went on calmly. "You're only making things worse, you know. How would you feel watching some stranger paw your sister?"

"I am not pawing!" he objected, looking even more wounded. He shot a glance at John's watchful eyes and then defiantly moved his hand back to its former place at the small of C.J.'s back. "And I'd like to know," he went on in a distracted voice, "how I'm supposed to keep my eyes and hands to myself."

C.J. giggled in spite of herself. "Bite the bullet," she murmured, and bit her lip in helpless amusement as he looked down at her reproachfully.

"Funny. You're a funny lady."

"I think so. Were you complimenting me, by the way, or was that meant to imply that you're a dirty old man?"

"I'm neither dirty nor old," he responded, sounding even more rattled as he intercepted an unfriendly look from Chris. "And I was complimenting you. I've been fighting a battle with all my baser instincts ever since you walked into the dining room. I'd like to throw you over my shoulder and carry you off somewhere."

"Why don't you?" She meant it to be a mocking question, but he immediately seemed taken by the idea.

"Shall I?" he asked, catching her left hand in his and drawing it up to his chest, a tiny fire kindling in his dark eyes.

"No," she said hastily.

"Coward."

"The guys would shoot you in the back," she explained sweetly.

"They'd be more likely to take me outside and thrash me," he said wryly. "Like gentlemen."

C.J. bit her lip again.

"And what's more," Fate added in a definitely aggrieved voice, "I'm supposed to be engaged to you. All nice and respectable. So why am I being treated like a cross between de Sade and Jack the Ripper?"

"It must be your honest face," she said politely.

"Uh huh. Really know how to cheer a guy up, don't you?"

"I try." Relenting, she said gravely, "Actually, their suspicion is quite understandable. They think you have villainous designs on my virtue."

"I have," he said. "Not villainous designs, but designs with honorable intentions. Don't they count for anything?"

"Not with big brothers."

"Great." Fate sighed softly.

Enjoying the sight of him rattled and off balance, C.J. was in no hurry to put an end to her teasing. "And then, there's always the natural mistrust of lawyers," she pointed out airily.

"Strike two."

"And then there's your name."

"What's wrong with my name?" he demanded, offended.

C.J. gave him a pitying look. "*Fate*. I mean, think about it. Gypsy fortunetelling with tarot cards and crystal balls; a tall, dark stranger, and all that. Destiny and luck. *Fate* . . . dark shadows and furtive looks. And so on."

"Strike three."

She couldn't help but laugh at his crestfallen tone.

He frowned at her. "Are we going to go on playing one-upmanship?"

"Is that what we're playing?" she asked innocently. "Then tell me—who's ahead?"

"You are. Damnit."

"At last!" She laughed again. "I'm finally one-up on the great Mr. Weston. Raise the flag!"

They had, by this time, entered the lounge. Music and laughter hit them with the force of a tide. The musicians were playing a medley of popular tunes suitable for slow dancing, and several couples were already on the floor.

"For heaven's sake, dance with me," Fate said rather hastily, as he glanced back over her shoulder. "They're coming toward us *en masse*, and I can't handle that. They can't object to dancing, can they?"

Of course not," she murmured, smiling sweetly as she went into his arms. "What's dancing, after all? Holding . . . touching . . ."

"Oh, hell," Fate muttered despairingly.

Six

C.J.'s giggle was cut short as a heavy hand fell on Fate's shoulder, and Patrick cut in with awful politeness. Giving way as gracefully as possible under the circumstances, Fate retreated to the refreshment table and gave C.J. a pathetic look.

Perfectly aware that he was mainly playing up to her enjoyment of the situation, she winked at him before Patrick swept her away, and had the satisfaction of seeing a glimpse of the little-boy mischief gleaming in his eyes.

"Now she's winking at the man," Patrick said high above her head.

C.J. tilted her head back in order to look up at her dancing partner, and couldn't help but laugh. "Well, don't sound so accusing," she reproved lightly. "Aren't I allowed to wink at a man? I've seen Kathy wink at you!"

"That's different," Patrick told her stoutly.

"Why?" she asked wryly.

He ignored the question. "C.J.—are you sure you know what you're doing?"

She looked up into concerned brown eyes, and realized suddenly how lucky she was to have friends who cared. Quietly, she said, "He's been good for me, Pat."

In the face of that statement, there wasn't much that Patrick could say. But he tried. "You barely know him," he objected.

"If I remember correctly," C.J. pointed out, "you proposed to Kathy on your first date—with all of us listening in. You didn't know her very well. Were you wrong?"

"In proposing? Of course not!" he denied immediately.

"Well?"

He smiled reluctantly. "Point taken. But, C.J., if you ever decide . . ."

"I'll give a shout," she said gently, responding to the question he couldn't seem to put into words.

"Good." He looked relieved. "As long as you know you can count on us." Looking over the top of her head, he added, "Here comes Brian for his turn."

"A policeman's third-degree," C.J. muttered. "Damn."

Patrick looked a little startled to hear her swear, but oddly tickled as well.

And then it was Brian's turn. Then Chris. Then John.

C.J. spent a good fifteen minutes responding to questions ranging from Brian's "What the hell are you up to, kid?" to Chris's "Why can't he keep his hands off you?" In between was John's mild, "What's this about parasites?"

By the time Keith claimed her for a dance, C.J. was trying desperately to keep a straight face. And the pathetic, beaten-spaniel looks Fate kept giving her every time she passed him weren't helping.

Keith caught that look as they passed. "Quite

an actor, your Fate," he murmured. "Very convincing."

Hoping that he was referring only to Fate's present actions, and not the loverlike attitude, C.J. murmured, "He really does want you all to like him."

"I know that," Keith said calmly.

C.J. smiled slightly. "I'm beginning to feel sorry for him."

"You didn't feel sorry during dinner."

So he *had* overheard, C.J. thought. Or guessed. "I was . . . having a bit of revenge," she said lightly. "Getting even with him for a personal difference of opinion." Before Keith could probe more deeply into the subject, she decided that the best defense was a strong offense. "What do you think of him? You haven't said much."

"No, I haven't said much, have I?" Keith looked thoughtful for a moment, then looked down at the grown-up little sister in his arms. "But now . . . I say God bless him—and the horse he rode in on."

It was such a strange thing to say, especially coming from Keith, that C.J. could only stare at him for a moment. Then she started to laugh. "May I ask why?"

He was smiling slightly, shrewd blue eyes studying her face. "Because he's brought you out of yourself. I hardly recognized you when you walked into the dining room tonight—and it wasn't because of the dress."

Choosing to take his words lightly, she mocked, "I'm all grown up now!"

With unwonted gentleness, Keith said, "It's obvious that he loves you very much. And you love him, don't you?"

C.J. took advantage of the sudden finale of the music to avoid answering him. But something closed down inside of her, something that was afraid of thinking about what he had said, something that was afraid of exploring a tender place.

She looked up at him as he began to lead her across the large room to Fate. "The others follow your lead, Keith, and you know it. Can't you get them to lighten up on Fate? I think he's suffered enough."

If Keith realized that she hadn't responded to his question, he didn't let on. Lightly patting the hand resting on his arm, he said, "I'll see what I can do." He said nothing more until they reached Fate, when he presented the small hand to the other man. "Your lady, I believe," he said gravely.

"I hope so," Fate said, his voice wary and dark eyes guarded as he accepted C.J.'s hand.

C.J. stared after the retreating figure with a warm smile, and then snared a glass from a passing tray before looking up at Fate. "Enjoying the party?" she asked innocently.

"Oh, sure, it's great. Just great."

Sensing that he was really disturbed about something, C.J. sipped her drink as she studied his face. It was the solemn Indian-face, she noted, and more somber than usual. "What's wrong?" she asked in an altered voice.

Fate didn't answer for a long moment, looking down at the small hand he still held. Then his eyes met hers, and she was surprised to see an unaccustomed frown there. Abruptly, he said, "You love him. I saw it in your eyes when you looked after him just now."

"Keith?" she asked, puzzled. "Of course I love him—I love them all." A sudden, bewildering thought struck her mind just then, and she nearly choked on her drink. "You're jealous," she said disbelievingly.

"Yes."

The flat, unequivocal response astonished her even more. While most men would have shown jealousy by brooding, possessive behavior, Fate quite openly and simply admitted to it.

And C.J. didn't know how to deal with that kind of honesty. She took a hasty sip of her drink and said, "You're stepping out of character, you know."

He ignored that. "Should I be jealous, pixie?"

C.J. looked fixedly at her glass. She wanted to tell him quite firmly that of course he had no reason to be jealous simply because he had no claim to her. But she couldn't say that . . . somehow. She lifted her gaze at last to find him staring down at her with anxiety in his dark eyes, and that look crumbled yet another defense.

"They're my big brothers, married to my best friends," she said quietly. "Nothing more than that."

"Should I be jealous?" he repeated softly.

She was aware that he wasn't acting now, aware that he was asking her to acknowledge a real relationship between them; she didn't want to do that. She was afraid to do that. But she could ignore the appeal in his eyes no more than she could have stopped breathing.

"No," she whispered at last. "No, you shouldn't."

He reached out to take her drink and set it on the table behind him, then removed the purse from beneath her arm and placed it there, too. "Dance with me." The purple eyes were glowing.

Silently, C.J. let him lead her out onto the floor, her arms slipping up around his neck naturally when he pulled her close to him and began moving slowly in time to the music. She rested her forehead against his chest, hiding her eyes from the ones that saw too much.

At a fork in the road, she thought dimly, and no

one to tell her which way to go. And yet, she had already taken a step. Her mind flew back to Keith's earlier observation and then tried to shy violently away. But that small mercy was denied her. What had closed down at Keith's words, his question, opened up suddenly now, and the revelation hiding there was painful in its raw awakening.

C.J. sighed raggedly without meaning to, and felt Fate's hands—warm on her bare back—draw her even closer.

"What is it?" he murmured into the curls tickling his chin.

She shook her head slightly. "Nothing." *Everything*! her mind added silently.

When had it happened? She wasn't sure. Even now . . . she wasn't sure. When a stranger had unexpectedly and cheerfully begun playing the lover? When a mischievous little boy had bent her over his arm à la Valentino? When a quickwitted, intelligent man joined with her in the verbal sparring she had discovered a liking for? When a sensitive, caring man told her about the struggle to save another man's life? When a man with desire in his eyes held and touched her?

She thought back to the first night, and suddenly had her answer. She had dreamed of an Indian, beautiful in his stark masculinity, tender beyond anything she had ever hoped for. He had touched her with cherishing hands, kissed her with adoring lips, murmured words of love in many languages.

Now, her fingers felt the softness of the raven-black hair at his nape, and she stroked it helplessly with unsteady movements. Yes. She had known then.

She had known then that she loved him.

C.J. heard the music stop, and she was aware of a panicky urge to run away and find somewhere small and dark and quiet. A place where she could think. A place where she could discover if this was reality . . . or insanity.

"C.J.?" Gentle hands turned her face up as her arms fell away from him, and a soft, rough exclamation escaped his lips. "You're white as a ghost! What's wrong, sweetheart?"

She looked up at him with blank eyes. And found that small, dark, quiet place—deep inside herself. Ruthlessly, she dragged the bewilderment, the nameless yearnings, the whirlpool of emotions into hiding and slammed the door on them. Until she could sort things out. Until she could think.

Conjuring a brilliant smile, she said lightly, "I need a drink." And she broke away from him resolutely to thread her way among the crowd of people to where Fate had left her drink.

He didn't catch up with her until she was lifting the glass for a second gulp. "C.J., what's wrong?" He grasped her arm and turned her to face him. "Tell me!"

"I'm a little tired and it's hot in here." Casually, she disentangled herself and then took his arm in a companionable grip. "Jan's waving at us; let's go see what she wants."

"C.J.—"

"You have to make friends with the guys, you know. The girls will be nervous wrecks for the wedding if you don't."

"The devil with them!" he muttered, moving toward her friends with obvious reluctance. "I want to know what happened between the beginning and the end of that dance."

Knowing that she barely had time to respond to his demand before they'd reach her friends, she said calmly, "Nothing happened, Fate. Nothing at all."

He had to be satisfied with that—for the time

being, at least. But C.J. knew very well that he wouldn't let the subject drop for long. She put it out of her mind, though, and hoped that she'd have an answer for him when the time came.

As soon as they reached her friends, who were grouped together near one of the fireplaces, the male half of the magic circle showed a tentative opening for Fate. Keith, having shed his reserve, casually asked Fate's opinion of a legal case involving a friend.

C.J. listened silently to the ensuing discussion, vaguely amused to note the first stiff-legged advances of the other men, still wary but apparently determined to offer olive branches. She didn't know what Keith had said to them, but it had obviously done the trick. The thaw had set in.

As soon as the men seemed absorbed in their talk, she slipped unobtrusively away. She exchanged her empty glass for a full one and then stood near the refreshment table sipping her drink and watching the group with quiet eyes. Not thinking. She wasn't ready for thinking yet.

Jan detached herself and came toward C.J. a few moments later. When she reached her, she said with relief, "Now maybe they'll stop acting like dogs protecting a bone."

"Thanks," C.J. murmured dryly.

"You're welcome," Jan responded politely, and then astonished C.J. by adding reflectively, "Not that I can blame them for being suspicious. That parasite-and-laser beam story was a bunch of bull."

C.J. choked and stared at her friend with watering eyes. "You mean you never—"

"Believed the story?" Jan grinned at her, unholy amusement showing in her blue eyes. "Of course not. With all due respect to Fate's convincing performance, he left out one very important explanation: why you agreed to keep meeting him

on the sly. That's just not like you, sweetie. Love
may have made you blind; it wouldn't make you a
fool. You'd have demanded an explanation, and
nothing less than the truth would have satisfied
you."

"Do the others know?"

"Sure. We're your friends, remember? We know
you." Jan frowned suddenly. "Or thought we did,
until this vacation." She searched her friend's
expressionless face and averted eyes, then said a
little dryly, "You didn't meet him two months ago."

C.J. silently mouthed the word "no."

Jan placed one hand palm down on the table
beside them as though to brace herself. "C.J.
—when you pulled him out of the hall and into
your room that first day . . ."

"He was as much a stranger to me as he was to
you," C.J. finished quietly, meeting her friend's
eyes at last with a glimmer of a smile in her own.

"My Lord," Jan exclaimed dazedly. "The chance
you took! Why, C.J.? To do something that reckless—" She broke off abruptly, shaking her head.

With a little shrug, C.J. looked down at the
glass in her hand. "It was stupid and reckless, I
know. I decided to invent a romance to stop all
the matchmaking. Only it backfired on me."

"You love him."

C.J. felt tears start to her eyes at the quiet
statement, and nodded jerkily. "Funny isn't it?
After all the years of your matchmaking, I fell in
love on my own." There was a certain relief in
admitting it out loud. Jan frowned at her as she
looked up.

"And you're upset about it. The man obviously
adores you. And you're still going to fight it, aren't
you, C.J.?"

C.J. wanted to avoid the question, but suddenly the fears and uncertainties burst loose from

their locked room. "Ever since that man charged into my life, I've been coming apart," she said in a low, hurried voice. "I don't know me anymore. I look in the mirror and a stranger looks back at me. It's all happening too fast, Jan. And . . . I'm afraid."

Surprisingly, Jan seemed to understand. "It hit you over the head like a ton of bricks," she said. "That's the way it happened to the rest of us. Someone once said that love doesn't ask, it demands. But you can't turn your back on it, sweetie."

C.J. shook her head suddenly. "It doesn't matter. Fate doesn't love me, and that's that."

"He says he's going to marry you."

"Part of the act," C.J. said tiredly.

Jan smiled oddly. "You're not listening, C.J. He didn't say that the two of you were going to get married. He said that *he* was going to marry *you*. There's a wealth of determination in those words. Don't listen to what a man says, listen to how he says it."

The advice made no sense to C.J. and she pushed it aside to ask a question which had been puzzling her. "If all of you knew that we were lying, why did you let the whole thing go on?"

"Are you kidding?" Jan lifted an amused brow. "Fate woke you up with a vengeance; a blind man could have seen that with his cane. We weren't about to throw a spanner into the works."

C.J. thought that over, her eyes fixed on the now animated discussion going on around the fireplace. "So you just stood around and let me make a fool of myself."

"No more of a fool than any other woman in love," Jan said coolly, responding to the accusation. "Don't be afraid of being foolish, sweetie; we all are at one time or another."

C.J. silently, wryly, agreed to that. She was, after all, being an utter fool. Fate *did* want to turn their charade into some sort of real relationship. Exactly what *kind* of relationship, C.J. wasn't sure. A vacation fling, probably. A brief affair before they went their separate ways.

And she was a fool because the reckless demon that had gotten her into this mess in the first place was now urging her insistently to take what she could get, even if that were only a brief affair.

A week, she thought dimly. In another week, she'd be back in Boston, and all of this would seem like a dream. Or a nightmare. She had less than a week to make up her mind. But that wasn't enough time—not for a rational decision.

A voice at her elbow recalled her attention suddenly, and C.J. looked up to find one of the ski instructors politely asking her to dance. He was handsome, seemed wonderfully uncomplicated, and was obviously much taken by the new image advertised by her dress.

Smiling brightly up at him, she accepted his invitation and set her glass back on the table.

"C.J.—"

She looked back at Jan as the ski instructor started to lead her away, and said. "It's a party, right?" Her voice was calm. Without waiting for a response, she added, "Well, I'm going to party!"

During the next hour, C.J. lost count of her dancing partners. She stayed as far away from Fate and the others as possible, flirting lightly with the men who clustered around her and trying steadily to drown her sorrows. In the back of her mind was the rather grim idea that if she made Fate mad, he would probably make her mad. And she felt safe on angry footing; anything else was treacherously unsteady.

Knowing from experience that the only change drinking stirred in her was a tendency to accept any challenge offered, she didn't worry about disgracing herself by becoming drunk. And she was perfectly capable of taking care of herself in the company of men who were out for what they could get.

The only problem was that Fate didn't get mad.

C.J. saw Brian start toward her once with a scowl on his pleasant face, and belatedly remembered all her big brothers and their protective attitudes. But then she saw Fate reach out a hand to stop the other man, saying something which was impossible for her to catch over the din of music and laughter filling the room. To her surprise, Brian—after a slightly puzzled look at Fate—apparently gave up his obvious intention of playing big brother.

Several graceful whirls by her partner just then enabled C.J. to catch a few glimpses of Fate. He looked neither angry nor jealous. In fact, the solemn Indian-face was completely unreadable as he watched his supposed fiancée having a grand time without him.

During the next hour, he calmly danced with nearly every woman in the room—with the exception of C.J. If her behavior disturbed him, he gave no sign of it.

And that accomplished a part of C.J.'s objective. It made her mad. She let the anger have full rein, channeling the other bewildering emotions into that handy outlet. Watching with jealous eyes as he danced with an obviously bleached blonde, she decided angrily that the last thing she needed in her life—whether as lover or anything else—was a two-faced Indian lawyer with rotten taste in dancing partners.

By midnight, C.J. was the life and soul of the party.

Recklessly, she accepted one challenge after another, from a vacationing businessman's request for a flamenco to the admiring ski instructor's desire to learn how to tango. She laughed gaily, flirted lightly, and refused to search for Fate in the crowded room. No one could have guessed that it was all an act.

He appeared magically out of nowhere sometime after one A.M. and calmly plucked her out of a noisy conga line.

She struggled to break the firm grip on her arm and found the struggle useless, and was angry to realize that she was being towed from the room like a misbehaving child. He had her purse in his free hand, and she had to hurry to keep up with his long strides.

"Damnit, let go of me!"

"No," he responded flatly.

Startled, C.J. looked up at him and discovered that appearances could be—and quite often were—deceptive. Expressionless face notwithstanding, he was furious.

It was yet another facet of the man, and C.J. was suddenly wary of this unsuspected side of him. As she stood silently beside him in the elevator, she felt ridiculously like a cross between a sulking little girl and a trainer whose sunny-tempered lion showed a sudden and alarming tendency to turn on her.

But there was also an odd expectancy within her, a curious tension she couldn't identify. She looked down at the firm grip on her arm as he led her down the hall to her room, and wondered vaguely why she felt no fear of his temper. No fear—only a deep and rather thoughtful satisfaction.

That was absurd. *She* was absurd. And where had her own temper gone to? Why was she no longer angry?

She didn't object when he halted in front of her door and released her arm to hunt through her bag for the key. And she watched silently as he unlocked the door, opened it, and gestured for her to enter. Still without speaking, she went in.

He tossed her bag onto the dresser and leaned back against the closed door as she turned to face him, his expression still unreadable. "Proud of yourself?"

The quiet question touched a raw nerve, and she felt her temper returning. "You're not my father or my brother," she said irritably. "Don't preach at me!"

He ignored her comments. "What were you trying to prove, C.J.? That you could bewitch every man in the room? You proved it. That you could drive me out of my mind by making me watch you bewitch every man in the room? You proved it."

C.J. turned her back on him, pacing over to the window and staring out, unaware that the blackened pane clearly revealed her strained face to the man behind her. He didn't sound as though he were out of his mind, she thought. In fact, she had never heard him sound quite so calm.

That should have warned her. It really should have.

She turned, feeling oddly defeated, intending to tell him to leave her alone. And found him two steps nearer and calmly dropping his tie on the dresser. When he shrugged from his black jacket and tossed it past her to land on one of the chairs, she suddenly found her tongue.

"What—what are you doing?"

Long brown fingers had the white shirt halfway unbuttoned. "You can't seem to make up your mind about me, pixie, so I think it's time I made it up for you."

His voice was casual, almost careless. But the purple eyes were gazing at her with an expression she instinctively recognized, and there was nothing even remotely casual in that look.

Like a rabbit in a snare, she found herself unable to move as he came to stand before her. But she was shaking her head dumbly, and finally managed to whisper, "No."

"Yes." Large hands rested on her bare shoulders briefly, then lifted to frame her face. "I've been as patient as I know how to be, but a man has only so much willpower. I can't take anymore, C.J. I need you so badly . . ."

The rough timbre of his voice, the note of unhidden longing, set flames racing through C.J.'s bloodstream. Silent and still, she watched as his head lowered slowly, blocking out the lamplight that cast a soft glow through the room. When his lips touched hers, her eyes fluttered closed, and a sigh came from deep inside her.

For a long moment, she neither fought him nor responded to him. Every muscle was tight as the sane, slightly cynical C.J. tried to ignore the sensations tearing through her body. But as his lips moved gently, sensitively on hers, cynical C.J. lost the inner battle.

With a mind and will of their own, her hands lifted jerkily, her arms slipped around his lean waist. Beneath her fingers, she felt the silkiness of his shirt and the firm muscled flesh beneath, and every silent, hard-won resolution shattered.

Fate deepened the kiss immediately as he sensed her blooming response, no longer pleading but demanding. He released her face to crush her fiercely against his hard length, his tongue exploring her mouth with the stark thrust of possession. He seemed ravenous in his need to go on kissing her, as though he had wanted to do this for a very long time.

She could feel the heat of his body burning her like a brand, adding fuel to the fire raging within her. Reckless excitement claimed her, seduced her, and C.J. no longer cared whether this was reality or insanity. It was what she wanted—needed—and that was all that mattered.

Fate's mouth left hers finally to plunder the soft skin of her throat. Hoarsely, he muttered, "Are you sure?" And then added immediately, "Don't say no, damnit!"

C.J. traced the rippling muscles of his back with a sort of wonder. "No," she said throatily, "but don't let that stop you."

A soft laugh escaped him. "I ought to leave you," he rasped, his teeth toying gently with a diamond-studded earlobe. "I should wait until you're sure—"

His reluctant statement ended in a groan as C.J.'s hands found their way beneath his shirt, her fingers teasing his spine. She felt a shudder pass through his body, and instinctively pressed her own even closer.

"Lord, I can't wait," he said thickly, his breath warm in her ear. "Tell me not to wait—not to leave you . . ."

C.J. felt his fingers slide up her spine, fumble with the fastening of her dress, and was suddenly desperate to rid them both of the barriers of clothing that separated them. "Don't wait," she said, unable to say anything else. "Don't leave me."

The clasp of her dress was released, the silky black material fell in a heap at her feet, leaving her nude but for the black sandals. He lifted his head to look down at her, glittering purple fire in his eyes. A strange, rough sound seemed to come from deep within his chest.

"You're so beautiful," he breathed almost inaudibly, the purple gaze sweeping over lamplit curves, shadowed hollows.

She had never in her life stood naked before a man, and C.J. was dimly surprised to find a shameless pride in his admiration. She felt no embarrassment, no discomfort. There was only a growing satisfaction that this man found her beautiful, a wild, sweet pleasure in the hunger in his eyes.

She pushed the white shirt from his shoulders, watching as he shrugged it away and let it fall unheeded to the floor. She felt oddly suspended, as though time itself had stopped and left this room and this moment the center of everything.

And she knew then that this moment had been planned, intended, from the second she had looked up into his eyes for the first time. Had it been sheer luck that she had recklessly chosen him to become her mystery lover? Or had it been destiny?

He had plucked her from behind her wall of abstraction within moments, teasing her, sparring with her. Awakening unfamiliar and nameless longings in her, teaching her to love him.

And the instant awareness between them had grown, building on itself for days.

She had wanted this, waited for it all week. It had been the driving force behind her sudden, feminine desire to make herself as beautiful as possible for him. It had not been temper which had caused her to buy the black dress; it had been him. He had awakened the woman in her, shown her the stranger in the mirror who was herself. And all week she had been preparing herself for this maiden voyage, this flight to test her wings.

C.J. kicked off her sandals as he lifted her into his arms and stepped over to the bed. He lowered her gently on the turned-down covers, before straightening and beginning to rapidly remove the remainder of his clothing.

And she lay still, watching him with drugged eyes, admiring the masculine beauty of strong limbs and powerful torso. Watching the thick black hair gleaming with blue highlights on his broad chest. Wondering dimly what it would mean to belong to this man . . .

Seven

When he lay down on the bed beside her, C.J. held out her arms to him. His eyes flared with some fierce emotion as he accepted the silent invitation, his arms gathering her close. Warm, curiously shaking lips rained kisses on her face, her throat. One large hand slid upward to cup a throbbing breast, and she moaned softly when his mouth closed over its hardened, aching tip.

Restlessly, her hands kneaded the muscle-padded shoulders, explored the hair-roughened chest. Her senses were filled with the scent of his cologne, the touch of soft hair and firm flesh, the dizzying feel of his pleasure-giving mouth. And somewhere near the center of her being, a coil wound tighter and tighter, filling her body with a sweet, mindless torture.

His hands were moving, caressing, shaping her body with the enthralling, rapturous touch of a lover. With infinite patience, moving tenderness, he learned her body as though this would be his only chance. As though he feared that eternity would claim them both, and he would have only this memory to sustain him.

The same need drove C.J. to learn what a man's body was all about. This man's body. Curiously, she explored with uncertain fingers, fascinated by hard planes and angles. Apparently understanding this moment of discovery for her, Fate shifted suddenly, rolling over to allow her the full scope of exploration.

"Touch me, pixie," he grated softly. "I need to feel your hands on me."

She hesitated for only a moment, raising herself on one elbow and meeting his fiery gaze a little timidly. But the encouragement shining in those purple depths gave her courage, and curiosity sparked an instinctive knowledge deep inside her.

Tawny eyes darkened almost to black as she leaned toward him, her fingers sliding slowly over his chest. Hesitation disappeared at the first tentative touch; instinct took over. She bent her head, her lips finding the flat male nipple among the dark hairs, and she felt his hands raking gently through her curls, sending pins flying.

His chest rose and fell rapidly beneath her touch, his harsh breathing audible. She felt his heart thundering against her, the beat keeping time with her own runaway pulse. Her hands slipped down over his flat stomach, feeling it quiver at the contact, hearing a hoarse sound that seemed torn from his throat.

Lying against him, she could feel the rigid desire burning against her thigh, and felt awed and staggered by the wisdom of a Creator who could design so marvelous a creature as man. With a need beyond reason, she raised herself suddenly, her hand moving lower still to touch the throbbing need he felt for her.

He shivered when she touched him as though her hand were a live wire, and then lay tautly still. Wonderingly, her fingers held him, caressing, inciting his body to ever greater response. Compelled by some fervent hunger unknown to her until this moment, she leaned over to touch her lips warmly to his pulsing flesh.

Dimly, she heard a rasping groan and felt him shiver again, but her attention was focused almost entirely on what she was doing. She wanted to give him pleasure, and nothing mattered to her except that. And then a giddy sense of vertigo swept her, and she found herself once more lying in his arms.

"Witch," he whispered between kisses. "Beautiful, enchanting pixie . . . how I need you!"

With growing urgency, he lavished her body with the touch of his hands, the hot, arousing brush of his lips. His caresses slid lower, over her breasts, her quivering belly, lower still. Reaching at last the warm center of her desire.

C.J. gasped aloud, the fingers gripping his shoulder going white with tension. Eyes wide and startled at this new sensation, she moved restlessly, the splintering, aching pleasure building toward an impossible peak. She was empty inside, hurting with this strange, sweet pain, and she needed him desperately.

"Fate!" She heard her breathless voice pleading with him, begging him to stop this sweet madness. And he rose above her, muttering words she didn't try to understand.

Her arms slipping up around his neck, C.J. gazed at him with hunger and infinite trust shining in her eyes, welcoming him in an embrace primal in its age and radiant in its sweetness. There was no fear in her heart, no hesitation, no shame.

He seemed to hesitate for a moment, his eyes drinking in the sight of her awakened, yearning face. And then his body moved strongly, joining them together, possessing her in a way that no man had ever done before, would ever do again.

She felt the breath catch in her throat, her wide, wondering eyes fixed on his taut face. And as he began to move, she moved with him, holding him, learning him. The tension shattered every nerve in her body, filled her senses until the world stopped in its orbit, ripping the sky with thunder, dissolving in rapture.

She cried out with the blissful agony, hearing Fate groan her name raggedly. His mouth found hers in that heart-stopping moment, sealing their union in a kiss of boundless tenderness.

The world gradually, slowly, reformed and went on its way, leaving two mortal beings to rediscover their earthly ties. But they were in no hurry. Indistinguishable murmurs fell softly in the lamplit room, bodies reluctant to lose this special closeness continued to lie closely together. Unsteady hands stroked dampened flesh, lips touched again and again like blind lodestones. And—characteristically—humor softened their gentle fall back to terra firma.

"What *are* you doing?" C.J. murmured plaintively as the shoulder she had pillowed her head on began to make earthquake-like movements.

"Getting the covers," Fate answered with a soft laugh. "I'm obviously going to need all my strength to deal with you, pixie, and I don't want to get off on the wrong foot by catching pneumonia."

He patted her hip before drawing the covers up around them, and C.J. reclaimed her former resting place with a sigh of satisfaction. "I should probably take exception to that remark," she reflected with a yawn smothered against his neck, "but I can't seem to."

"Ah! I've found a way to shut her up!"

She punched him weakly in the ribs.

"Don't hit your lord and master, you little pixie!"

"Listen to the man. He takes advantage of a poor, defenseless woman and then caps off his villainy by not even allowing her satisfaction. S'terrible. Just terrible."

"I got her drunk, too."

"She got herself drunk. Not that I was. Drunk, I mean."

"You're getting your tenses all tangled up."

"No, just my pronouns."

"Whatever."

"Do you make mistakes like that in the courtroom?"

"Constantly."

"Doesn't bode well for the arm of the law."

"Who's the lawyer here?"

C.J. smothered another yawn. "Beats me." Then she squeaked. "*Now* what're you doing?"

"Guess."

She batted his hand away. "You're not decent!"

"I need something to hold on to," he protested, wounded.

"Well, not that."

"Why not? You have a spare."

"*Fate!*" She choked and fought to swallow the giggle. "Is this what they call pillow talk?"

"Certainly."

"Dinner table conversation is a lot cleaner."

"That's because lovers have a conversation not intended for other ears," he informed her loftily.

"Like this one?"

"Exactly." He gasped suddenly. "What are *you* doing?"

"Guess."

"Witch! If you don't stop that, you'll find yourself seduced for the second time tonight."

"Oh, was I seduced? I wondered what that was. There I was, minding my own business, and you started taking your clothes off."

"You offered insupportable provocation."

"Really?"

"Yes. You taught that ski instructor how to tango."

"Oh."

"Don't do it again."

"Is that a command, Mighty Chief?"

"Yes. And what's with the mighty chief bit?"

"I think of you as an Indian."

"Blood will tell," he said.

"You mean you *are* an Indian?"

"Three-quarters Sioux, I'm told. As a matter of fact, I was named after an Indian ancestor. My father had already decided that I'd follow in his footsteps, and he thought the name would be very apt for a lawyer."

C.J. thought that over. "What's the other quarter?"

"English."

"Oh."

"Are you going to walk three paces behind me?"

"Only if we're walking on thin ice."

"Thanks."

"You're welcome."

"While we're being polite," he said casually, "may I ask how you've managed to escape the clutches of a man for twenty-six years?"

"The first sixteen years don't count."

"The last ten, then."

"No one would have me."

His arms tightened slightly, and when he spoke, his voice was husky and not at all casual. "Then the men you've known were blind and stupid. But I'm glad. I'm very glad, pixie."

C.J. was surprised and somehow touched to realize that it did matter to him. There was a thread of awe in his voice, as though he felt that she had given him a precious gift. Moved by that, but unwilling to have him speculating on her reasons, she managed lightly, "I'm very inexperienced; you'll have to teach me."

He chuckled suddenly. "You have a great deal of natural aptitude, believe me." He seemed to understand that she needed humor, lightness.

His hand felt around under the covers, zeroing in like a homing pigeon.

"I thought I told you to stop that."

"When they put me to bed with a shovel."

"Quit it before you start something you can't handle!"

"Oh-ho! That's touched my pride!"

"Fate, stop it! We'll be dead for the wedding! Fate? I don't trust the look in your eyes! Stop that . . . what're you? . . . I don't want to . . . Oh, hell. . . ."

A long time later, C.J. barely found the energy to open her eyes as Fate turned out the lamp on the nightstand. "I just don't see," she managed to murmur, "how the Indians lost any battles. I'll bet Custer ran into someone like you at Little Big Horn."

"Napoleon must have met you at Waterloo. . . ."

The sporadic ringing of a bell interrupted C.J.'s blissful sleep, and she opened her eyes reluctantly to gaze sleepily at a day-lightened ceiling. Lazily, her mind toyed with the meaning of the disturbing bell, finally coming to the conclusion that it was the phone. With a sigh, she started to roll over and answer the shrill demand.

But there was a heavy, unaccustomed weight across her middle. Immediately, the night before came back to her in great detail, and she turned her head slowly. For a long moment, no longer paying attention to the phone that continued to ring, she stared at the handsome, sleeping face half hidden in the pillow beside her own.

But the sound apparently got through to Fate. With a groan, he rolled over to fumble for the receiver. Eyes tightly shut, he finally managed to uncradle the thing and then rolled back to her side and buried his face back into the pillow. "What?" he demanded in a muffled voice, the receiver to his ear.

Amused in spite of herself, C.J. watched as one dark eye opened and fixed itself on her face. There was puzzlement in the purple depths for a moment, then a tiny fire kindled. He handed her the phone, his arm returning to its earlier resting place and his face nuzzling into her neck. "For you," he said.

"Thank you," she said politely.

"Don't mention it." His lips found an earlobe and began toying gently.

Trying to ignore a little shiver of delight, C.J. brought the receiver up to her other ear. "Hello?"

"C.J.?"

She wanted to giggle at the rattled sound of Jan's voice, but bit it back. "Hello, Jan." Apparently, she decided, surprise at a little sister's coming of age wasn't limited to big brothers.

"Should I inquire into the state of your virtue, or just gracefully allow the subject to drop?" Jan asked wryly.

"Let it drop. Is that why you called?"

Jan sighed. "No, of course not. Do you happen to know what time it is?"

"Can't see the clock," C.J. murmured dreamily, tilting her head slightly to allow wandering lips to explore her throat.

"It's noon."

"Noon!" She sat up abruptly, dislodging Fate who protested audibly. "But the wedding's at two!"

"Yes, well, I wondered if you remembered that," Jan responded affably. "Do you think you could desert the lovenest long enough to participate? Kathy's sort of counting on you and Fate, you know. Of course, if you're too busy . . ."

"We'll be there. Don't start without us." C.J. leaned over Fate to replace the receiver, cutting off Jan's laugh. Fate pulled her completely on top of him and drew the covers up around them both, with all the air of a man making himself comfortable.

"Carolyn Jennifer," he murmured, nibbling on her chin.

"My word, the man doesn't even know my name!" she accused in a shocked voice, temporarily putting aside the urgent matter of getting ready for a wedding.

He sighed, his fingers threading among her curls in order to pull her head down for a kiss. "I should have caught you last night while you were weak with passion," he declared. "You would have told me then."

"Why didn't you?" she breathed, catching his lower lip teasingly between her teeth.

"I was too weak with passion to think of it," he confessed.

C.J.'s soft laugh trailed away as she felt his hands slide beneath the covers and begin moving over her back in a disturbing way. "We have to get up," she protested reluctantly.

The purple eyes were smiling up at her. "I love you, you know."

She felt a curiously hot-cold chill shoot through her body, felt her heart begin to pound with a wild rhythm. He loved her? But that wasn't possible; it didn't make sense! There was nothing special about her; she was too ordinary for a man like Fate to fall in love with her.

But maybe he felt that a declaration was obligatory? That after their night together, she would need to hear the words, however false they may have been?

Before he could prevent her, C.J. had rolled away from him and sat up, looking pointedly at the clock. "We have less than two hours to get ready for the wedding," she reminded him lightly. "We'd better get a move on."

"C.J.?" He sat up, too, one hand catching her arm when she would have slipped from the bed. "You don't believe me, do you?"

Continuing to strive for lightness, she asked, "Does it matter?"

"Damnit, of course it matters!"

She shook her head slowly, feeling the sting of absurd tears in her eyes and not knowing why.

His free hand reached out to grasp her chin, turning her face gently until she met his eyes. In an altered tone, he asked softly, "What are you afraid of, honey?"

"I don't know," she whispered. "Fate . . . it's all happening so fast. I—I don't want to think about tomorrow. I feel—new. Raw. As if I'm beginning all over again. I need time to get used to that."

Fate searched her uncertain face for a long moment, then leaned over and kissed her softly, sweetly. "All right," he said huskily. "But I'm going to do my damnedest to convince you that I love you. Don't deny me that right."

"I wouldn't think of it," she managed, torn between laughter and tears.

He brushed a single tear from her cheek, then caught her in a fierce bearhug. "Just don't cry," he groaned. "I can take anything but that!"

A hiccupping little laugh escaped her, her sense of humor coming rapidly to the fore. "Can't stand to see a woman cry, huh?"

"Any other woman, I probably could. But not you. It tears me to pieces." He sighed roughly. "You don't seem to realize it yet, honey, but I'm putty in your hands."

Surprised at the wry admission, she watched as he slid from the bed and began to dress. Hugging her upraised knees, she let her eyes drink in the sight of him. "Aren't you taking an awful chance by telling me that?" she asked softly.

"Maybe." He shrugged into his white shirt, and then leaned over to kiss her one last time. "But you see . . . I love you."

"You're not playing fair," she whispered.

"I'm not playing at all. I'll give you as much room as I can, C.J., as much time as you need." He straightened and picked up his jacket and tie, going toward the door. Then he hesitated and looked back at her. "Just don't expect me to be quiet about how I feel, love. I want to shout it from the rooftops."

C.J. barely heard his promise to return to pick her up as soon as he'd changed. She stared almost blindly at the door for a long moment after he had gone, feeling the sudden emptiness of the room like a physical blow. Then she slid from the bed and headed for the shower.

Why hadn't she responded to his admission of love with her own love for him? The thought haunted her as she showered automatically. Fear. What was she afraid of?

It came to her slowly as she was dressing that she had not voiced her love aloud because by doing so she would be committing herself. Putting a name to her feelings would be to admit that they were real, and she still wasn't sure. In spite of everything that had happened, everything they had shared, she was still raw and tender from the newness of her emotions.

Independent all her life, emotionally alone in spite of the friendship of the magic circle, she wasn't sure how to open herself fully to another human being. And the very thought of that kind of vulnerability frightened her.

What if it didn't last? He would take away a part of her; she would lose something that she could never get back, never replace. Nothing would ever be the same again. . . .

But nothing will ever be the same again now, a little voice inside her head whispered.

She shied away from the thought, realizing abruptly that trying to get everything clear in her mind now was like probing a raw wound with rough hands. Just as she had told Fate, she needed time. She would take one day at a time and try to understand what had happened to her. Try to find out whether or not her relationship with Fate was real and would last.

That resolve enabled her to greet him calmly when he knocked on her door sometime later. "Good—you can zip me up," she informed him, catching his hand and pulling him inside the room.

"I'd rather unzip you," he countered cheerfully.

"Funny man." She presented her back. "The wedding starts in half an hour; Kathy's probably spitting nails."

Obediently, he pulled the zipper of her dress up, dropping a kiss on the nape of her neck when he had completed his task. "You look beautiful. That rustly stuff is very becoming."

"This 'rustly stuff' is chiffon," she said, moving over to the dresser to pick up her bouquet. "And thank you." She glanced down at the floor-length dress, colored a soft pastel yellow, and then looked appraisingly at his tuxedo. C.J. allowed her eyes to wander over him slowly, from the sleek black hair to his gleaming shoes. Hastily, she swallowed the lump in her throat. "We'd better go."

They were silent as they made their way to the chapel on the top floor of the lodge. But, oddly enough, it wasn't an uncomfortable silence. Fate held her hand firmly, looking down at her from time to time with a smile. And C.J. couldn't help but respond to the warmth of that caressing look.

She wondered vaguely if she would look different to her friends, then dismissed the thought as fanciful. But she would have been astonished to have been told just exactly how different she appeared. All five of her friends immediately noticed the change in her from the moment Fate opened the door of the small room just outside the chapel and led her in. Though there were still shadows of uncertainty in her tawny eyes, her face was radiant, and her fingers twined with Fate's in an unconscious gesture of trust and devotion.

"At last!" The bride, surrounded by her attendants, swung around to confront the tardy couple at the door. "So you finally decided to come?" She swept forward, detaching Fate from C.J. and shoving him toward the door. "You can hold hands with C.J. later—right now go next door and help the guys give Patrick their moral support. I think he's going to turn chicken on me and run."

Laughing, he was shoved out the door. C.J. found herself the cynosure of all eyes as soon as the door was closed, and managed a faint, rueful smile. "Hi," she offered brightly.

"Just one question," Jan said amiably.

C.J. gave her a guarded look. "What?" she asked warily.

"Have you eaten lunch?"

Surprised, C.J. started to laugh. "I haven't even had breakfast," she confessed.

Jan gestured toward a table in one corner. "Well, since we don't want you fainting during the ceremony, help yourself." She nodded at the tray of canapes resting on the table. "Kathy got the munchies a little while ago, so Tami went down and raided the buffet."

C.J. moved to the table. "I thought brides were supposed to refuse all sustenance due to nerves," she said, with a sidelong, teasing look at Kathy.

"Not practical ones," Kathy retorted dryly. "Jan, this veil isn't right. I think you put it on backwards!"

"Don't be ridiculous. I've put on five veils, friend, including my own. I should know how to do it by now."

"Well, it isn't right!"

"It's fine. Susan, what did you do with the garter?"

"It was here a minute ago. I gave it to Tami—"

"And I gave it to Ann."

"C.J., you're sitting on it!"

"Sorry."

"Kathy, don't sit down, you'll crush your dress! Just stand there; I can get the garter on."

"Whose wedding is this, anyway?"

"Yours, and don't be difficult. There! Something borrowed. *And* something blue. The bracelet Patrick gave you, that's something new. And you have your grandmother's pearls for something old."

"Can I get married now, mother?"

"Oh, shut up! I was the first to marry, so naturally I have to make sure the rest of you do it right."

"Naturally."

"Here are your flowers. I meant to ask, by the way, why we're all carrying different flowers. Your bridal roses are traditional, but what about the rest of us?"

Kathy grinned. "I wondered when somebody'd ask! If you'll remember, I chose the flowers months ago—and I chose them very carefully. You're carrying goldenrod, which means 'encouragement' —little mother Jan! Susan is carrying laurels, which means 'glory.' " She lifted a brow at beautiful, regal Susan. "For obvious reasons."

Susan inclined her head slightly. "Thank you."

"You're welcome. Ann is carrying China asters, which means 'I will think of thee.' She's the most loving of us all."

Ann smiled, her violet eyes showing pleasure at the tribute.

"Tami is carrying coreopsis, which means 'love at first sight.' I've never seen anybody fall as hard as she did for John."

They all laughed, and then Jan lifted a questioning brow. "What about C.J.?"

"Well, now, there I lucked out." Kathy turned brown eyes brimful of laughter to the sixth member of their group. "C.J.'s carrying coral honeysuckle—which means 'color of my fate!' "

"Good Lord," C.J. said faintly.

A maverick in most matters of tradition, Kathy had planned a wedding which was both simple and traditional. That was, aside from a chorus of five voices exclaiming "We do!" when the minister asked who gave this woman in marriage.

C.J.—who had been oddly moved by walking up the aisle beside Fate—paid unusually close attention to the vows exchanged at the altar. Having attended both the weddings of her friends and the wedding of her sister, she had heard the words many times before. But never before had they touched her so deeply.

She glanced back once at the crowded chapel, seeing the solemn faces of fellow guests at the lodge, most of them strangers to her. Their presence was mute testimony to Fate's belief that everyone enjoyed weddings, and C.J. decided that apparently all the world *did* love a lover.

Listening to the words that were heavy with the weight of ages, watching the two serious, glowing faces of the couple standing tall before the minister, she wondered how anyone could doubt the future existence of weddings and married life. As long as the human heart could look to the future with hope, there would be weddings. As long as men and women met and fell in love, there would be weddings.

C.J. felt an odd quiver go through her at the thought, an elusive fear which darted too rapidly to be caught or even seen. Unwilling to probe for the truth, she hastily turned her mind back to the ceremony. And heard the happy couple pronounced husband and wife.

Since Kathy wasn't one to stand on her dignity, and since the magic circle was an effusive group, there was an immediate rush for the altar once the ceremony was duly concluded. Pandemonium reigned for some time, and then the bridal pair was borne on a tide of good wishes to the buffet set up downstairs in one of the dining rooms.

C.J. found Fate close beside her as they waited their turn for the elevator, and a warm feeling stole through her when he caught her hand and held it firmly.

"At last!" he murmured into her ear. "It's a funny thing, but I seem to get withdrawal pains whenever I go too long without touching you. You've obviously bewitched me, pixie."

"Pixie's don't bewitch," she informed him calmly, "they enchant."

"Same thing."

"Not at all. Bewitching suggests witchcraft, which suggests black cats and boiling caldrons and spells. Enchantment, on the other hand, suggests elves and fairies and magical kingdoms and wizards with stardust."

"I stand corrected."

"Very gracious of you."

"Nice of you to notice."

"I'm a noticing kind of woman. As a matter of fact, I've been meaning to tell you that I read minds. But I was afraid that it would scare you off. Does it?"

"Of course not," he denied stoutly. There was a short silence, then he asked uneasily, "Do you really read minds?"

"Certainly." C.J. stepped into the elevator as the doors slid open, fighting to keep her face solemn. "It's a rare talent, you know. Not everyone has it."

"What am I thinking right now?" he demanded suspiciously.

"That I'm a liar."

Fate drew her nearer in the crowded elevator. "Bingo! What do you know—she *does* read minds!"

"It's a gift."

"Give it back."

"Funny, Maestro. Be careful, or I'll give you back."

"Was I a gift? I think I should resent that. Who gave me?"

"Your namesake."

They joined the others making their way toward the dining room, and he took a moment to respond. "You mean fate?" When she nodded, he went on cheerfully, "Well, that's all right. I don't mind being given to you—by whomever or whatever."

"Gosh, it's all mine! What shall I do with it?"

"Take it to your heart and cherish it," he directed firmly. "Don't feed it candy or let it chase cars. And pat it kindly on the head from time to time. A little tender loving care."

"Yes, but what does it *do*?" she asked gravely. "I'm not much for useless ornaments, you know."

"It's good in courtrooms," he offered hopefully.

"I don't know about that. It got its tenses and pronouns mixed up."

"One little mistake!" he exclaimed, hurt.

She ignored that. "And it has an unnerving habit of acting a little crazy. I mean, I'm all for being my brother's keeper, but that bit of sage advice wasn't meant to be taken literally."

Fate pulled her suddenly into a handy alcove just outside the dining room and out of the way of traffic.

"Why are we stopping?" she asked severely.

"Well, *it* has to show what *it's* good for, doesn't *it*?"

"Fate, you wouldn't!"

He would. And did.

Emerging from the embrace totally breathless and feeling that at least three ribs had been cracked, C.J. said weakly, "That's quite a talent you have there."

"I hoped you'd appreciate it," he murmured.

"Well, don't look so smug, damnit!"

"I don't look smug, I look satisfied," he said

with injured dignity. "I want you to be satisfied with the package, after all."

"How can I be satisfied with a bundle of dynamite and a match?" she asked wryly.

"Some people like to live dangerously," he noted.

"Sure. Some people like to jump out of airplanes, climb mountains, and hunt lions. Happily, I am not one of their number. I'm much addicted to safety and comfort."

"That's no fun!" he objected reproachfully.

"It may not be fun," she said stubbornly, more than half serious, "but it's a lot more calm."

In the tone of one clinching an argument, Fate said, "You told Patrick that I was good for you."

"Hearsay, counselor," she retorted instantly. "Not admissible as evidence."

"Then here's some firsthand evidence—I make you laugh. Admit it!"

"Bob Hope makes me laugh. So does Murphy's Law, old Tarzan movies, feathers, and letters from the Internal Revenue Service."

"Well, if that last isn't living dangerously—"

"Also fat puppies, talking birds, and kids," she finished dryly.

"And me," he added calmly.

"You come in somewhere between the fat puppies and the talking birds," she said reflectively.

He ignored that. "I'm good for you; admit it. I keep you on your toes and make you laugh."

"What you do," she replied, "is make me doubt my sanity."

Instantly, she was caught in another bearhug. "At last! The woman made an admission! I'm driving her crazy. That's step one. Now for step two."

C.J. tried to hold back as he began leading her toward the dining room, but her efforts at resistance were unsuccessful. "What do you mean step two?" she demanded suspiciously. "Fate, what have you got up your sleeve *now*? Fate? Fate, are you listening to me?"

"No, darling; you aren't saying anything important."

A bit shaken by the endearment, C.J. nonetheless pushed on. "I want to know what you meant by that!"

"Be patient. You'll find out soon enough."

"But what do you *mean*?" she wailed.

Eight

What Fate meant turned out to be quite an experience for C.J. She was neither a shy woman, nor easily embarrassed, and the past week had somewhat accustomed her to public displays of affection. After all, Fate had played the lover like one born to the role.

However, compared to the Fate who had declared his love and meant to prove it, that earlier Fate was a total slouch.

If C.J. had been asked to define a true romantic courtship, she would have instantly produced as an example the days of knights and chivalry. Days when a man had adored his chosen lady openly and constantly, writing poems, singing songs, performing brave deeds. When tenderness and sensitivity had been virtues, and honesty had been more than just a word. Idealistic, perhaps, but no woman could think of that age without a tug on the heartstrings.

And C.J. would have added other qualities from other ages in history that she admired. The grace-

ful compliments from Regency England. Lovely
rituals from the Orient. The gentle courtesy and
fierce protectiveness of the ante-bellum South. And,
being a woman, she would have added a smatter-
ing of caveman rough-and-ready tactics—just to
keep things lively and interesting.

Realistically, of course, the grave deeds that a
twentieth-century man could perform for his lady
were few and far between. And Oriental rituals
required at least a passing acquaintance with the
countries in that geographic area. Poetry, also,
required at least some innate skill, and a bit of
practice.

The rest demanded a man, simply, who was
neither afraid nor ashamed to show the softer
side of himself. A man who openly and cheerfully
declared himself to be in love and loving it, without giving a particular damn who was watching
or what they would think of him. A man who
seemed to see rainbows around every corner complete with pots of gold, and castles in the air, and
clouds with silver linings. A man who could make
love gently and with great tenderness, then turn
abruptly and revert to primal man, filled with
fiery passion and raw need.

A tall order. But Fate filled it.

He might have taken a page from C.J.'s book
and read her mind. Or he might simply have been
drawing on the love of history that both of them
shared. Perhaps both. Then again, it could have
been the natural outpouring of Fate in love.

Whatever it was, C.J. was by turns amused,
moved, excited, bewildered, astonished, and delighted by the courtship.

The wedding celebration lasted—predictably—all
day and well into the evening. The bridal pair

disappeared sometime in the middle of the festivities, and no one was tactless enough to go looking for them. They were hardly missed, on any account. The buffet turned into dinner, which turned into a full-scale party with dancing and whatever. Nobody bothered to change, but ties were loosened and flowers discarded.

Fate danced with C.J., staring daggers at anyone who even *looked* as though he were going to cut in. He kept her laughing with his energetic sales pitch for the package fate had tossed into her lap, enumerating his qualities—all good—which ranged from a protective love of animals to a total lack of vices such as snoring.

Sandwiched between the catalogs of his virtues were sessions during which he pulled her into various dark areas and continued to demonstrate to her what "it" was good for. By the time they left the party sometime around midnight, she would have fought like a wildcat if he'd even suggested she should sleep alone. Not, of course, that he did.

He delighted her that night. Wooed and seduced her. With ardent tenderness and spellbinding gentleness. He was the Indian from her dream, murmuring words of love and need in many languages and taking her to a place only angels and lovers knew of. He made love to her as though that act and that moment in time were the only things that mattered. The center of everything. And waking up beside him the next morning gave her a feeling of completion and contentment she had never known before.

And that day began to give the word "courtship" a whole new meaning for C.J.

It started with a shared breakfast in bed—carried in by a poker-faced waiter—and then went on to a shared shower. Rapidly discovering that Fate couldn't look at her or be near her without touching her, C.J. surprised herself at the total lack of self-consciousness and embarrassment within her. She found that she not only enjoyed the little touches, she returned them. And the teasing between them continued.

"Why didn't you tell me you spoke several languages?"

"You didn't ask."

"Oh. You know, I had a funny dream the night we met."

"Did you?"

"Yes. Um . . . Fate?"

"What, sweetheart?"

"Stop nibbling; I want to ask you something."

"Go ahead. I can nibble while I listen."

"My neck is not caviar! Besides, I can't see your face."

"Your neck is better than caviar. Put that soap down, you little witch! All right, now you can see my face. What's the question?"

"That dream I had . . ."

"What about it?"

"It *was* a dream . . . wasn't it?"

"How should I know?"

"Fate?"

"What?"

"Never mind. I don't think I want to know."

"Whatever. My turn now."

"Your turn for a question? What is it?"

"Cyrena Jasmine?"

"Sorry."

"Clorinda Junella?"

"Heavens, no. Where *are* you getting these names?"

"I found a book. Cosima Jacosa?"

"That can't be a name!"

"Well, it is."

"It's not mine."

"Damn. Take pity on me?"

"No. It amuses me."

"Cruel. Why do I love you?"

"Beats me."

"I'd like to."

"How creative! Right now?"

"In a minute. When I finish nibbling."

"I thought you were finished."

"When pigs grow wings."

"I read a story just the other day about a pig with wings."

"Don't believe everything you read."

"The water's getting cold."

"I'll keep you warm, love."

"Funny man."

"Chryseis Joakima?"

"Sorry . . ."

After the shower, and feeling unaccountably energetic, they decided to go skiing. C.J.'s friends made no appearance, either having been prompted by him, or showing unexpected tact. Most of the other guests were apparently sleeping off last night's party, so C.J. and Fate virtually had the slopes to themselves.

He challenged her to a race down one of the more advanced slopes, won by an indecent margin, then gloated so loudly that she caught him off guard and pushed him into a snowdrift. Nose in the air, C.J. executed a beautiful kick turn, dug her poles in, and glided away.

He caught up with her a few yards away, tackled her gently, and covered her with snow and kisses until she surrendered and apologized. In a masterful tone, he demanded that she plead to be allowed to get up, and was answered with snow down his neck.

By the time the tussle ended, they were both covered with snow and gasping for breath. By mutual consent, they left the argument in the air and decided to repair to the lodge for lunch. After the meal, over which they conducted a spirited discussion on the rival merits of football and hockey, Fate took her into the deserted lounge and sat her down at one end of the couch.

"Wait here."

"For what?"

"You'll see."

Curious, she sat before the fire and stared into it, smiling to herself. What Fate had in mind, she didn't know. But she was thoroughly enjoying his company, so it didn't really matter. She was a little surprised, though, when he returned to the room carrying two mugs in his hands and a small hardbound book under one arm.

"Hot chocolate," he explained, handing her a mug.

"Thank you," she murmured, and then watched in amusement as he placed his own mug on the coffee table, then stretched out on the couch with his head in her lap.

"Comfortable?" she asked politely.

"Luxuriously," he replied with a gusty sigh. He propped the small book on his chest and opened it.

"Am I boring you?" Her voice was affable.

"Not at all. I'm going to read love poems to you. It's called wooing. Pay attention, now."

Oddly touched, C.J. sipped her chocolate and gazed at his grave face, listening to his deep, rich voice read words written in celebration of love centuries before.

It was about half a dozen poems later that she suddenly felt the heat of the fire transfer itself to her cheeks. "Good Lord," she said faintly. "What *is* that?"

Fate looked up at her solemnly. But there was laughter in the purple depths of his eyes. "A love letter. From a poet to his wife. He'd been away from her for months."

"It sounds like it," she said involuntarily. "I've never heard anything so—so—"

"Earthy?" he suggested gravely. "I believe I've said it before, but you're cute as hell when you blush."

She gave him a goaded look. "Take my advice and don't say things like that when you're at my mercy. I could drown you in chocolate."

"Hush. You're being wooed."

"It sounds like I'm being invited to do something illegal."

"Would I do that?" Rather hastily, since she showed definite signs of answering a resounding yes, he added, "Shall I read the wife's reply to the letter?"

"Is it as bad as his letter?"

"Worse. Women can be earthy, too."

"Oh. Well, I'm not interested."

"Liar."

She held her mug over his head, tipping it threateningly. "Don't push me, Maestro."

"I was commending your taste," he said reproachfully. "This stuff is considered classic literature, you know."

"Really? Oh, well, who am I to scoff at culture? Read on."

"Sure you don't want me to spare your blushes?"

"Sure you don't want a chocolate facial mask?"

Bowing meekly to the threat, he began to read again. Moments later, C.J. was laughing.

"My God, you were right! That's worse than the first one was!"

"Or better, depending on your point of view," he said critically. "They were perfect for one another, weren't they?"

"Sounds like it."

"Like us."

"Read on, Mighty Chief."

"You're a stubborn lady, pixie." He sighed heavily. "But I love you anyway. Let's see now . . . the next poem . . ."

The wooing continued that day. And the next day, and the next. The nights were filled with the kind of loving most women don't even dare to dream of, covering the entire spectrum from gentle tenderness to lusty desire. C.J. never knew whether she would be softly wooed and coaxed like a reluctant virgin or attacked by a lusty Indian brave and ravished delightfully.

She woke one morning to find that her brave of the night before had transformed himself into a troubadour . . . or something. He was sitting cross-legged at the foot of the bed in glorious nudity and strumming a guitar that had come from heaven only knew where. And singing love songs.

Not even his sleep-mussed hair and morning stubble could detract from his smooth baritone, and C.J. listened with sleepy pleasure. Until he began to sing a sailor's ditty which would have made the poet and his wife blush; then she hit him with a pillow.

He got back at her later that day by challenging her to a game of chess and then whispering sweet nothings to her across the table until she could barely concentrate.

"Stop that. You're distracting me," she said, moving a pawn decisively.

"And you're distractingly beautiful," he replied softly, moving a knight almost absently.

"Ha!" She moved another piece quickly. "What do you think of that, Maestro?"

He smiled at her across the small table. "I think that was a bad move, love." With only a glance at the board, he made his own move. "Checkmate."

"Damn!"

"Want to try again?"

"Only if I can gag you!"

"Temper, temper . . ."

She challenged him to a game of strip poker later that night in the privacy of the room they now shared, confident in her ability to win the game her uncle had taught her. But once again, Fate proved that it wasn't wise to bank on anything where he was concerned.

Wearing only a blanket and a glare, C.J. flung down her final hand. "Three aces!"

"Sorry, sweetheart." He didn't sound it, and certainly didn't look it as he showed her the flush in his own hands. "The blanket has to go."

"It's all I've got left!"

"The blanket."

"You wouldn't want me to catch a cold."

"The blanket."

"I think you cheated on that last hand."

"I've decked men for less. The blanket."

"Have you really? Decked men, I mean?"

"I'm a basically violent man. The blanket."

"You're a basically crazy man."

"The blanket."

She threw it at him. Of course, she had to be punished for that. And one thing naturally led to another. The Indian brave was back, and C.J. thoroughly enjoyed the visit.

How the remainder of the magic circle spent the last days of their vacation, C.J. didn't know. Nor did she particularly care. If they were smart, she decided, then husbands and wives would be together and sharing the kind of closeness that she had discovered with Fate. But that was certainly their affair.

Day by day—literally hour by hour—C.J. found herself falling more deeply in love. She felt that she had known Fate forever, and that he knew her better than anyone ever had before. There was something very seductive in that—and something that was also frightening.

Still, she wasn't ready to take the final step and admit that she loved him. Fear was definitely a large part of her reluctance. At times, she felt she could almost grasp that fear, almost shake it and find out what it contained. But then her mind would shy nervously away, prefering to live for today and not for tomorrow.

It puzzled her, this reluctance to face herself. She had never been conscious of it before. That her relationship with Fate was responsible for it, she knew. But what was there about their relationship to frighten her? His love? That didn't frighten her—it astonished her. She still found it difficult to believe that a man like Fate could fall in love with her. However, it would have taken a harder heart than hers to resist his wooing.

Her love? It was certainly a powerful and somewhat unnerving emotion. People had killed for it, died for it. Written songs and poems and books about it. Attempted to explain it away, or laugh it off, or deny it. Debated it and scorned it.

What love did to people! There were examples in the history that she loved. People driven to madness and murder, to suicide. People gambling everything on it, joyous when they won and despairing when they lost. People wandering the world in search of it. Queens resorting to trickery to achieve it. Kings abdicating for it. Ordinary people driven to extraordinary feats because of it.

And there were, of course, all the different facets of love. A mother or father's love for a child. The love of brothers and sisters. The love of friends. And the thousand-and-one other kinds of love: of ideals, of country, of animals, of dreams.

And the strongest love of all, the love between a man and a woman. Some called it chemistry. It made saints of some and sinners of others. For some it was filled with romance, for others with tragedy. It lifted one to the very heights of ecstasy and dropped another to the depths of despondency.

What had it done to C.J.?

Constantly in Fate's company, she had very little time to examine the question. But she considered it from time to time. Love had made her a stronger person, she thought. No longer on the outside looking in, she was now aware of life and living through every pore of her body. Her senses seemed to have opened up, showing her the sights, sounds, tastes, scents, and touches of a world she had only dimly seen before.

Love had shown her the value of laughter, the wonder of the passionate side of her own nature. It had sharpened her wits and stirred her mind and awakened her body.

Awakened . . . Love had awakened her.

There was nothing to be afraid of in that, surely. Of course, she was no longer insulated, protected, by her own indifference. But Fate was there. Instinct told her that if she were required for some reason to walk through hell, Fate would take her hand and walk by her side, sharing the journey for good and bad. She would not have to ask him, he would demand. He would say it was his right and his responsibility, because he loved her.

Then why—*why*—couldn't she admit her own love aloud? It didn't make sense! What was she afraid of? That his love would die as quickly as it had been born, leaving her adrift and alone? No, she was willing to take that chance.

Why was she afraid?

Between and around these questions and speculations, the wooing continued.

And the pillow talk between them taught both things about themselves and each other, not the least of which was the fact that they were so mentally attuned to one another that it bordered on telepathy.

"What are you doing, pixie?"

"I'm trying to find—oh, there it is." Her voice was muffled beneath the covers, until she emerged with a diamond earring held in one triumphant hand. "You made me lose my earring; I'll never find the back, it's too small."

Fate took it away from her and placed it on the nightstand, immediately drawing her close again. "Never mind. You look just as beautiful with only one earring."

C.J. snuggled up to his side, blinking sleepily in the lamplight. "You're very good with the blarney," she observed, one finger absently tracing an intricate path through the hair on his chest.

"What blarney? I'm not Irish, and I'm not a flatterer. I'm an old cynical lawyer, my love, and I'll thank you to remember that. I have a cold, analytical mind and a skeptical nature."

"Is this the man who woke me up with a naked serenade?"

"Certainly."

"That's very paradoxical, you know."

"Not at all. Human beings," he said instructively, "are made up of contradictions. Take yourself, for instance."

"You just did."

"Don't be crude, brat." He made her squeak by swatting a delightfully rounded buttock.

"Sorry."

"So you should be. Where was I?"

"You were implying that I'm contradictory."

"Right. And you are. When we met, you were almost completely hidden behind a very thick layer of bland inoffensiveness."

"That's an odd choice of words."

"But apt. You told me yourself that your friends had been needling you for twenty years. You took it because it didn't bother you in the slightest. You watched everything that went on around you with very detached interest."

"I have a feeling that you're about to attribute a drastic change in me to a slightly crazy Indian brave."

He ignored that. "I had never met anyone with a better defense system. And the fascinating thing was that it wasn't deliberate. You weren't hiding from anything, and you weren't afraid to let your emotions run free. You had maintained an unusually close friendship with five other women for twenty years, and had been immediately adopted by the men in their lives; that in itself shows a large capacity for affection and understanding."

C.J. listened intently with the slightly surprised interest which one usually feels when another person reveals insights into one's own character.

"You were highly intelligent, innocent, without being naïve, and utterly and completely unself-conscious. You were wrapped up in your work and studies, but not lost in them. And yet—I think—the only time you ever truly came out of yourself was when something or someone offered you a challenge."

Oddly unsurprised at his perception, she murmured, "So I'm a mass of contradictions."

"You certainly are. And there's something fascinating about contradictions, you know."

"Tell me about it," she said wryly, thinking of his own impossibly contradictory nature.

"Then, of course, came the catalyst."

She punched him in the ribs. "I knew it! You're going to pat yourself on the back for that, aren't you?"

"Ha! Then you admit that there's been a change in you since I came along!"

"Nonsense," she said loftily. "If I've changed at all, it's because I was ready to change. You just happened to be standing around when it occurred, that's all."

"Deny the fact that after twenty years of needling from your friends, it only took twenty minutes for me to get under your skin," he challenged.

"At that point, it only needed one last straw, and you were it," she responded coolly.

"Do you realize how much you've changed in less than two weeks?" he asked reflectively, ignoring her denial.

"No. Tell me." Her voice was mocking, but she was interested in hearing more of his surprising insights.

"The protective layer is gone, for one thing. Your emotions are closer to the surface. You're quicker now to laugh or get mad. You don't feel guilty any longer for ignoring your studies for a little while. And the warm, passionate side of your nature has been allowed to break free. Do you know, by the way, just how utterly delightful you are in bed, pixie?"

"Thank you," she said politely.

"You're entirely welcome."

"I'm a quick study, I suppose?"

"Very quick. You seem to have had a great deal of natural aptitude. One of your ancestors must have been a courtesan."

"Fate!"

"That's an honorable profession in some places."

"Not where I come from."

"Sorry," he mumbled.

"And how you can have the nerve to say something like that when I'm being attacked every time I turn around—!"

"Not attacked—" he protested.

"Yes, *attacked*! Last night, I was attacked in the shower, and I had soap in my eyes. And yesterday morning, you kept six people waiting in the lobby because you'd pushed the stop button and attacked me in the elevator. You even attacked me on the ski lift, and *that* was a sneaky trick, because I couldn't very well get away!"

"You love it," he said confidently.

"You're utterly insane, Maestro."

"Let's hear it for insanity, then. I've never been happier."

A little startled at the seriousness of his voice, C.J. traced an even more intricate pattern on his chest and murmured, "Really?"

"Good Lord, haven't I convinced you of that, at least?"

"You *seem* happy, but . . ."

"But what?"

She moved restlessly at his side. "You seem to think there's something special about me, and I don't know what that is."

He was silent for a moment, one hand lightly stroking her arm and the other playing absently with her copper curls. Then, in a quiet voice, he said, "You take yourself too much for granted, sweetheart. When I'm with you, I have everything I've ever wanted, everything I've ever dreamed of."

"But—"

"I wasn't lying about what I told the girls that first night," he went on in a whimsical voice, ignoring her interruption. "You looked up at me, your beautiful eyes startled and wary, your lovely face and hair and body hinting at the vital, passionate woman you were . . . and I felt as if the roof had caved in on me. And during the next twenty minutes, I found out everything else I needed to know.

"Your mind was quick and lively. You were intelligent and humorous and oddly vulnerable. You were obviously self-confident in your abilities, calmly sure of yourself. You had a quick temper, but not a cruel one."

C.J. listened wonderingly, bemused by what he was saying, by the certainty in his deep voice.

He sighed a bit roughly. "I'd given up on finding someone like you, pixie. Someone that I could laugh with and fight with and love. I could see that you weren't interested in any kind of a relationship, that you had your future planned and there was no niche in those plans for a man. I was desperate to find some way of spending time with you, to make you aware of me. And then the idea of continuing with your mysterious romance hit me. I knew it was risky, because you would naturally think that I was acting. But I had to take that chance. I needed to be close to you."

"Hoist by my own petard," she managed shakily.

He chuckled softly. "You could say that. I could see that I had gotten under your skin at least a little that first night, so I kept trying. I was so convinced that we belonged together that I couldn't understand why you didn't see that, too. Then, when I got to know you better, I realized that you were afraid of something. Can you tell me what that is now, sweetheart?"

C.J. made another mental grab for that elusive fear, and missed again. "No," she whispered. "I don't know what it is. I know it's there, but I can't see it clearly."

He gave her a brief hug. "We'll work it out. I've waited too long for you to give up easily, honey." Then, apparently realizing her need for laughter to chase away the fear, he went on lightly. "I'll even be very un-macho and admit that it doesn't bother me in the least that you know more about history than I do."

"You know more about law," she pointed out, welcoming the change of subject.

"A dull subject."

"And you play the guitar and sing."

"I read poetry, too," he said with a self-congratulatory tone.

She giggled. "And very nicely."

"I'm a whiz at chess."

"You distracted me."

"I excel at poker."

"You cheated."

"You're only saying that because you're a sore loser."

"No, because I got very cold without my blanket."

"Not for long."

She sighed sadly. "You took advantage of me. You're *always* taking advantage of me."

"The Lord will get you for that."

"For what?"

"Lying through your teeth."

"He'll get you for taking advantage."

"How can I take advantage of what's mine?"

"What d'you mean *yours*?"

"Mine." His hands began wandering beneath the covers. "All mine. And I'll fight to the death anyone who says otherwise."

"Then grab your bow and arrows, Chief! You—"

"Possession is nine-tenths of the law," he pointed out calmly.

"I was seduced entirely against my will. Possession doesn't count in that case," she informed him huffily.

"You were unwilling, huh? Then tell me, unwilling lady, who woke me up this morning with a definitely lewd suggestion?"

"It was not!"

"Was, too."

"Well . . . the poet must have rubbed off on me."

"Excuses, excuses."

"I seem to remember definite enthusiasm on your part."

"I didn't want to hurt your feelings."

"Oh, yeah?"

"Certainly. A gentleman, I am."

"You're an unscrupulous, conniving, deceitful lawyer-actor-Indian with not an ounce of truth in you!" she declared roundly.

"Talk about blanket condemnations!"

She squeaked. "Fate, what're you—? Stop that!"

"I've got a lewd suggestion, pixie."

"No, really?" she demanded with awful irony. "I wonder why I didn't guess that?"

"Don't you want to hear what it is?"

"I shudder to think."

"I'll make the suggestion anyway." He pulled her over completely on top of him and began whispering in her ear.

"The poet rubbed off on you, too," she said.

"Well, pixie?"

"Well what?"

"What do you think of my suggestion?"

"I think it's a good thing the door is locked . . ."

Nine

"Caledonia Jinx?"

C.J. pulled her sweater into place and sent an amused glance at the man sprawled out lazily on the bed. "Not even close. And where, by the way, is that book you mentioned? The one with names? I haven't seen it yet, but you seem to have memorized every name beginning with a C or a J."

"That's exactly what I did. And sooner or later I'm bound to hit on the right combination," he said, ignoring her first question.

"Not at the rate you're going."

"Have patience. Or tell me your name."

"No."

He sighed. "Then at least tell me why you're disgustingly wide awake at the crack of dawn. And why you're abandoning me."

C.J. sat down on the foot of the bed to put on her shoes. "It may have escaped your notice, but I haven't had a close encounter of the third kind with the great outdoors in two days. And since you said you had to make a few phone calls this morning, I thought I'd take a walk. You know—putting one foot in front of the other and staying upright?"

"That's a novel idea."

"Not original, I'm afraid. It's been done for years."

"Really?"

"Certainly. Your average, reasonably sane person makes a practice of it. You wouldn't know about that, though."

"Don't insult the mighty chief. He'll make you braid your hair and walk three paces behind him."

C.J. rose to her feet and lifted a haughty brow at him. "My hair's too short to braid, and I've already pointed out the only time I'd walk three paces behind you."

"Sass!"

"Well, if you were looking for meek obedience, Chief, you've got the wrong body."

"Oh, no," Fate murmured, linking his fingers behind his neck and gazing at her from beneath sleepy lids. "I've got the right body, all right. Pretty little thing. She even shaved me yesterday morning."

"Don't let that go to your head," C.J. advised calmly. "I was just getting in a bit of practice with a razor. One never knows when knowledge like that'll come in handy."

"Hemlock, I think, is easier," he said judiciously. "You'd better marry me first, though. The insurance, you know."

"Oh, I don't need the money." Her voice was serene. "I'm very rich."

"In that case, you have to marry me. I can't believe my luck—falling in love with a woman who's beautiful *and* rich."

C.J. knew very well that he thought she was joking, the way she had been about reading his mind. She wondered vaguely what his reaction would be when he discovered the truth. She wasn't particularly concerned and dismissed it. "The only things I *have* to do are pay taxes and die eventually."

He sighed again. "You're just not treating my proposals with the gravity they deserve."

"Gravity," she said thoughtfully, "makes apples fall to earth. It isn't much good for anything else."

"I propose and she lectures," he said ruefully.

"Sorry."

"I'm getting used to it, pixie, And don't you dare leave without kissing me goodbye."

C.J., who had started toward the door, paused and looked back at him with a frown. "Oh, no! I've discovered the dangers of getting anywhere near that bed while you're in it."

"You make me sound like a sex maniac," he complained.

"Maniac. Period." She went to the closet and took out a thickly quilted jacket. "Anyway, I'll only be gone an hour or so."

"Where's my kiss?"

She blew him one.

"Poor substitute for the real thing," he grumbled.

"Make your calls," she countered unfeelingly. "I'll be back in a little while."

Very softly, he murmured, " 'In my life there was a picture, she that clasped my neck had flown; I was left within the shadow sitting on the wreck alone.' " When she looked puzzled, he added casually, "Tennyson."

Staring at the solemn Indian face she loved so much and knew so well, C.J. felt a lump rise in her throat. She wanted to fling herself into his arms. To hell with her stupid, elusive fears! What other woman would hesitate to accept the wonders Fate offered? Not many . . . unless they were totally insane.

Like she was.

But C.J. knew rationally that she had to be sure. She had to be able to give all of herself, the way Fate did.

"See you later," she managed at last. But his voice stopped her at the door.

"There's another quotation."

She stopped and turned slowly to face him. "What is it?"

"Shakespeare. 'That I should love a bright, particular star and think to wed it.' Marry me, pixie."

It was quiet, almost a plea, and C.J. couldn't summon a light response. He was sitting up in bed now, looking absurdly endearing with his mussed hair and morning stubble. The covers had fallen to disclose his bare chest, and one uncovered—and muscular—thigh hinted at the bare rest of him. And her throat ached with love for him. Her voice would emerge only in a whisper.

"I'd like to marry you," she said honestly, but held up a hand when he would have slid from the bed. "I want to marry you. But I have to straighten out a few things in my own mind. Can we—can we talk about it when I get back?"

He nodded, saying huskily, "I'll even settle for a definite possibility of a firm maybe."

She laughed shakily. "Oh, you have that already."

His purple eyes were glowing. "It's a start." Then he added roughly, "Get out of here before you get attacked."

She turned back to the door, unlocked and opened it, then glanced back over her shoulder one last time. "I'd miss that if you stopped. Attacking me, I mean."

"No fear of that, love. When the world ends, I might stop. Then again . . . I doubt it."

The image of him sitting there in her bed remained with C.J. all the way down the hall to the elevator. And even when she pushed it from her mind, similar images took its place. A solemn face with dark eyes narrowed à la Valentino. A naked troubadour strumming a guitar and singing love songs. A gentle lover; a ravishing Indian brave; a humorous companion.

It was Thursday; tomorrow afternoon, she was due to board a plane to Boston. Her home was there, and her job, and her studies. And her friends were there.

And Fate's life and work were in Denver. What, she wondered wryly, were they supposed to do—pick a halfway point at which to live? Peoria, for instance. Halfway between Denver and Boston. They could both commute on weekends.

Great . . . just great. A weekend marriage. Oh, she could afford to fly back and forth every day, but what kind of marriage would they have? And her accountant would certainly do more than wince at the yearly bill.

Would Fate leave Denver for Boston? C.J. wasn't sure. He was a partner in a law firm, and heaven knew partnerships didn't grow on trees. However, her shrewd business sense told her realistically that it would be a hell of a lot easier to move one lawyer to Boston than to uproot an entire corporation and head westward.

It was a major problem, but it touched C.J.'s mind only lightly and briefly. She had complete faith in their ability to work out a concrete, soluble problem such as that.

It was the little elusive ones that bothered her.

"C.J.?"

Stepping out of the elevator in the lobby, C.J. automatically shrugged into her jacket and looked toward the entrance to the dining room in surprise. Jan was coming toward her.

"Hi, stranger!" her friend sang out wryly as she neared.

"Morning." C.J. shoved her hands into her pockets and stopped where she was. "You're up early."

"And you're up—amazing! We were beginning to think that you two had gone into permanent hibernation. Where's your Fate, by the way? Or is that an indelicate question?"

"He's upstairs," C.J. answered noncommittally.

"Mmmm. Is he heading back to Boston with us, or are you planning on Denver?" Jan's question was casual, but her blue eyes were intent on C.J.'s face.

C.J. shrugged. "We . . . haven't made any firm plans."

"Leaving it a little late, aren't you? I know you don't have to be back at work until the middle of next week, but—"

Shaking her head, C.J. cut her off. "There's a board meeting at the company Monday afternoon; I have to be there."

"You missed the last board meeting," Jan pointed out.

"I can't miss this one. The board's talking merger, and I won't have all the facts until I talk to them. Steve'll probably be there to represent Siri's interests since the doctor doesn't want her to travel during the last month of her pregnancy. He'll side with me, I know, since it's what Siri wants. If I decide against the merger, we'll have to pool our family stock to veto it."

"It's a pity Fate isn't a corporate lawyer," Jan said ruefully. "He could advise you. Does he know about the company, by the way?"

C.J. shook her head, smiling slightly.

"Well, isn't it about time you told him? I mean, I don't know of many men who'd balk at marrying a woman who virtually owns one of the largest companies on the East Coast, but it's not exactly something you want to whisper into his ear on the way to the bridal suite!"

"True." C.J. sighed softly. "And heaven only knows how he'll react. Talk about a dark horse! He's never the same twice out of the gate. I think he's part leprechaun and part chameleon." She reflected for a moment, then added, "And part troubadour."

"Troubadour?" Jan asked quizzically.

"Private joke." C.J. moved restlessly. "I'm going for a walk, Jan. I'll see you later." She turned and headed for the door, but Jan's voice halted her only a few steps away.

"C.J.? There's no problem is there? Between you and Fate? You look a little upset."

Turning back, C.J. hesitated for a moment. The lobby was empty; even the desk was deserted. And weren't friends supposed to help when one was unsure? "Jan . . . were you afraid—before you married Brian?"

Apparently realizing that the question was a very serious one, Jan answered quietly. "Of course I was afraid; I was marrying a policeman. Not the safest job in the world."

"But that's understandable—that's a concrete fear. I mean, were you ever afraid without knowing the reason for it?"

Jan was silent for a moment, then nodded. "I was giving up a part of myself to someone else, and that was scary. I didn't know what that meant for a long time, but when I finally understood, it wasn't scary anymore."

"And what does it mean?" C.J. was unaware of just how forlorn she sounded, how young and uncertain.

Her friend smiled. "It means that you get back

more than you give—much more. It means that there's always someone beside you, propping you up when necessary. You're never alone, even when you're by yourself. There are words you never have to say, thoughts you never have to voice aloud. It means that someone sees you in a very special way, a way no one else sees you." Jan's smile widened. "It's nothing to be afraid of, C.J."

C.J. let her friend's words sink in for a moment, then nodded as if to herself and made her way out the door of the lodge. Once outside, she zipped her jacket, casting an absent glance up at the heavy gray sky. She started walking, paying no particular attention to where her steps led her.

Was she afraid of giving up a part of herself to Fate? C.J. thought about that for a while, realizing almost immediately that it wasn't that she was afraid of. As wonderfully open as Fate was, she wasn't the least bit afraid that she would give only to remain empty.

Tangled thoughts and questions chased one another through her mind. She was afraid. What was she afraid of? She wasn't afraid of love. Marriage didn't frighten her, since the examples before her all her life had been happy and content ones. She trusted Fate, completely certain that he would never deliberately hurt her. She wasn't afraid of losing her independence, or becoming a possession.

Apparently, there were a lot of things she *didn't* fear. Which was terrific. But why, then, couldn't she tell Fate that she loved him and would willingly— gladly—marry him?

"Because you're an idiot, my girl," she said to herself, watching as another early-morning riser crossed her path shouldering a pair of skis. She flipped a mental coin, then turned in the direction of the ski shop. Exercise—that's what she needed. Exercise and fresh air. To clear the cob-webs away.

Moments later, she left the ski shop, poles and skis in hand. She had only half heard the talk inside about a prediction of uncertain weather due to hit today. Continuing to brood, she took the lift to the highest slopes, flipped another mental coin, and finally set off in a direction she hadn't previously explored.

C.J. paid little attention to where she was going, other than to avoid obstacles such as trees that were directly in her path. She wasn't worried about becoming lost; an excellent sense of direction had always stood her in good stead. Nor was she aware of the passing time. It was only when the rumbling of her empty stomach became too uncomfortable to ignore that she stopped long enough to look at her watch. And surprise kept her still.

Four hours! Well, no wonder she was both tired and hungry! She glanced back in the direction she'd come from, and felt suddenly very alone in the stark emptiness of the white, still landscape. *Idiot! You're miles from the lodge, and didn't even bring a candy bar!* And she had told Fate that she'd be back in an hour . . .

She sighed and looked around absently, her gaze picking up what looked like a tiny cabin tucked away in the woods about a hundred yards away from her. It looked deserted. Incurably curious, C.J. headed in that direction.

Five more minutes wouldn't matter, she reasoned. Besides—she wanted to sit down for a little while.

The cabin was indeed small, though apparently well-built, and most certainly deserted. The snow around it was pristine, no footprints—or hoof-prints, or pawprints—marring its beauty. And when C.J. tried the door hesitantly, she found it unlocked. Offering mental apologies to whoever owned it, she opened the door and stepped inside after removing her skis.

Two unshuttered windows on either side of the door allowed the single large room to be flooded with light. A wooden table with two chairs occupied the center of the room. One wall boasted a stone fireplace, three generous-sized logs stacked neatly on the grate. A second wall was lined with a narrow counter with cabinets overhead. What appeared to be a portable kerosene stove sat on the counter.

And the third wall, surprisingly, was mostly taken up with a wide, somewhat tarnished, brass bed. From the sway in the bright quilt covering it, C.J. deduced that the springs sagged decidedly in the middle. In spite of that, she hastily squashed an impulse to lie down and take a nap.

A slightly dusty appearance convinced her that if someone lived here, they'd been absent for a while. Yet the place seemed to have been left conveniently ready for stray, slightly weary travelers. A kerosene lamp and a box of matches sat on the table, firewood was stacked in one corner, and there were handy pegs on the wall by the door on which to hang one's coat.

C.J. glanced at her watch and bit her lip, undecided. But the lure of that fireplace was finally too strong to resist. She could build a fire and rest for an hour or so, she thought. It would be an easy matter to put out the fire—with snow, or something. Then she'd be rested and ready for the trip back to the lodge.

Feeling suddenly very, very tired, C.J. brought her skis inside and closed the door, going immediately to the fireplace. Within moments, she had a cheery fire blazing, and the cabin was beginning to warm up. Leaving her jacket on for the time being, she explored the cabinets, surprised by the amount of foodstuffs stored there.

What was this place, she wondered, a gift from the patron saint of tired skiers? There were first-aid supplies, a supply of kerosene for the lamp and stove, every possible kind of canned goods—and two dusty bottles of wine. C.J. checked the label on one, and raised a silent, appreciative eyebrow. Well! The patron saint was a generous soul; this stuff was older than she was.

Putting the bottle back, she continued her exploration. Pots, pans, other cooking utensils, and—two of each—plates, cups, forks, spoons, knives, and wine glasses. C.J. blew the dust off one of the goblets and shook her head with a smile.

From the looks of it, she'd stumbled on a lovers' rendezvous. Fancifully, her romantic mind wove a story of star-crossed love and secret meetings. She peopled the story with villainous parents and a noble pair of lovers, mentally pitting them against one another and casting every possible obstacle in the path of true love.

Giggling to herself, she located a jar of instant coffee—a bit stale—and made several trips outside the front door before melting enough snow over the kerosene stove to make coffee. When it was ready, she poured some in one of the cups and sat down at the table, lifting her cup in a toast.

"Here's to you, kids," she murmured to the silent room and her noble couple. "And I certainly hope you haven't planned an assignation for today—or there's apt to be a bit of a crowd!"

Her amusement faded as she sipped her coffee and stared into the crackling fire. Absently, she removed her jacket and draped it over the other chair, her mind turning from the mythical troubles of her noble couple to the very real troubles of herself.

She was being, she decided, an utter fool. There was no earthly reason why she shouldn't marry Fate and live happily ever after. He was everything she'd ever looked for in a man.

Looked for?

C.J. smiled wryly as she remembered all the years of matchmaking. Oh, yes . . . she'd been looking even then. Even through the veil of disinterest, the layer of abstraction. Searching for her perfect mate. And didn't all women do that, even if only subconsciously? In spite of independent proclamations, and assertions of self-sufficiency, and don't-give-a-damn aloneness . . .

She had watched her friends go through it. How complaisant they had been at eighteen, how confident and certain of what they meant to do with their lives! And how raw. None—with the possible exception of Ann—had thought of love or marriage or children. They were going to shake the world, they were. Rock it back on its heels and make it take notice.

Instead . . . Five weddings floated lazily through C.J.'s mind. Five women who had grown up and fallen in love. Five men who seemed quite happy to have married, not world-shakers, but women.

So the world had not been shaken—did that matter? No. It mattered only that five women had found their ideals, and were happy. They had fought their way through the thoughts and ideas of a fierce generation, and emerged triumphant.

And C.J.?

Not vehement like Jan and Kathy, merry like Tami, regal like Susan, or serene like Ann. C.J. had watched and listened, moving from one challenge to another, indifferent outwardly and restless inside. Shrewd in business, but not intrigued by it. Fascinated by history because there was so much of it, so much to learn.

And searching . . . always searching. History had fed her curious soul. Business had briefly and occasionally stirred her lively mind. One sport after another had engaged her interest for a time before passing unheeded and unregretted from her consciousness.

Feeling suddenly excited, C.J. realized that she was getting very close to her fear. Think! Tie it all together. She got up to put another log on the fire and refill her coffee cup, then returned to her chair.

All right. Use the examples she knew—the magic circle.

Jan. What had she needed most in the man she would marry? She needed someone who would take care of her. "Little Mother" Jan, who had watched over them all for years. And Brian filled that need; he was protective, calm, dependable.

Kathy. Fierce, sarcastic Kathy. She had needed a calming influence in her life, a sensibility to check her impetuosity, a cheerfulness to temper her sarcasm, a gentleness to soften her sharpness. And she had found each quality in Patrick.

Tami. Laughing, merry Tami, who could find something funny in everything. Always the clown, the court jester. She had needed a man who would see the more serious, gentle side of her nature. A man who would not be satisfied only with the quips, the one-liners, the jokes. And John had fallen in love with the woman beneath the laughter.

Susan. Beautiful, regal Susan. With her queenly air and striking, impossible beauty. She had needed to be seen beneath the mask of classical beauty. Hers had been, perhaps, the most difficult task. For a man to see beneath her mask, she had been forced to open herself up, and that had not come easily to cool, restrained Susan. But Chris had been patient, and his reward had been a woman who knew that she was loved for her inner beauty.

Ann. Gentle, loving Ann. She had withdrawn into frozen despair after the tragic loss of her first love. What Ann had needed, more than anything else, had been security. She had been afraid to love again, terrified of giving her heart only to lose it. But Keith had become her last and strongest love. He had given her the roots she had craved, loving her with a deep and enduring love. He was her shelter, her prop, her anchor in the wind. And she adored him.

And C.J.?

Ruthlessly, C.J. placed herself in the objective light under which she had examined her friends.

C.J. Something of an introvert. Accustomed to observing rather than participating. Inwardly restless, inwardly hungry. Always looking, searching. Needing a challenge, something to spark her mind and catch her attention. Easily bored.

And she needed . . .

Easily bored. Challenge.

Fate. Unconventional, paradoxical. Fate, who was ten men rolled into one. Intelligent, quick-witted, perceptive. He could delight her with verbal fencing, move her with tender wooing, excite her with lusty passion. He could have her in stitches with his pillow talk one moment, and then reach down deep inside her and touch places she didn't know existed. Not afraid or ashamed to be everything that a man could be: tender, humorous, passionate, silly, lusty, gentle, comical, cheerful, serious, absurd and endearing . . .

Attacking her blissfully in showers and elevators, on ski lifts. Singing love songs naked. Solemnly reading slightly obscene love letters and poems.

Holding her hand with the cheerful abandon of a teenager. Making love tenderly, and passionately, and lustily.

As changeable and unpredictable as the sea . . .

Her cup hit the table with a muffled clatter as C.J. stared toward the fire in amazement. And only the crackling fire and the empty room heard her disgusted voice.

"C.J. Adams, you are a fool. A total and complete idiot! The damn thing's been staring you in the face, and you didn't have the sense to see it!"

A *challenge*! That's what she needed so desperately—a man who could challenge her on every level. Fate. And her stupid, elusive fear was the fear of losing that challenge. She was afraid that boredom would creep over her, the restless urge to move on to something new.

But that wouldn't happen with Fate!

Propping her forehead on one hand, C.J. stared down at the rough surface of the table and muttered unprintable descriptions of her own intelligence. A gypsy with a crystal ball could have seen the truth quicker than she had, for heaven's sake! Ruefully, she was aware that Fate had unwittingly aided her in being blind for so long.

That first week had been bewildering and unnerving. She had found herself pitchforked into the middle of a torrid romance with no idea of how to play her part. And Fate's unpredictable behavior—though definitely catching her interest—had only made things worse. She had believed that he had been acting and, in doing so, had felt no desire to examine her own motives.

And this last week . . . Almost constantly in his company, being wooed delightfully, she had had precious little time or energy to wonder what was going on inside her own head.

Now, C.J. felt a sense of overpowering relief

flood her. No man could have played a part so well, or for so long. Fate was Fate—ten men rolled into one—and she would never have to worry about becoming restless or bored with him. There would always be another facet to be explored, another layer of the man to be absorbed and fascinated by.

He would always stir her mind and excite her senses. Irritate her, amuse her, move her, slightly bewilder her. Make her laugh and think and cry. Make her whole for the very first time.

Characteristically, C.J. was suddenly almost frantic to race back to the lodge and fling herself at him. Smother him with kisses. Seduce him. Woo him, damnit! She had an awful lot to make up for; he had made himself vulnerable to her, and she had said not word one to assure him that he would not suffer for his openness.

Jumping to her feet, C.J. hastily grabbed a large pot and headed for the door. She'd put out the fire with snow, leave the cabin as she'd found it, and make tracks back to the lodge as fast as her suddenly energetic legs could manage. She'd tell him that she loved him and would be *delighted* to marry him, and then—

The thought was never completed. Flinging open the door, she paused on the threshold, staring outside. Snatches of conversation she'd only vaguely heard in the ski shop suddenly etched themselves in her mind like neon signs.

"Forecasters are predicting a storm by noon. . . . Looks like it's going to be a real monster. . . . Haven't had a real blizzard around here in years— guess we're due for one. . . . Don't stray too far away, now, you never know . . ."

"Oh, no . . ." C.J. breathed softly.

Snow was falling in huge, fat flakes. The fall was not heavy at the moment, but the sky had darkened to slate gray, and wind was beginning to stir the tops of distant trees.

"Damn. Damn, damn, *damn!*" C.J. closed the door slowly and leaned back against it, staring blindly at the interior of the cabin. No matter how anxious she was to get to Fate, she was *not* fool enough to go charging off into the middle of a blizzard. It was miles to the lodge, and she hadn't left a trail of breadcrumbs. And even an excellent sense of direction could become muddled in a storm.

She wasn't particularly frightened by the possibility of being forced to spend as much as several days here alone. There was food enough; the wood in the corner would last through the afternoon and coming night, and she had noticed that a woodshed on one outside wall of the cabin held at least a three-day supply of cut logs. And, if worse came to worse, she could always employ the hatchet she had discovered in one of the cabinets to chop up the table and chairs.

The mental image that last thought left failed to bring a smile to C.J.'s face. What she was concerned about was the fact that no one at the lodge would know if she was safe. Her friends would be frantic, and Fate . . . She didn't like to think of Fate's reaction.

She glanced at her watch and frowned, feeling suddenly uneasy and more than a little frightened. For Fate. She had been gone from the lodge for slightly more than five hours; it was quite possible that he had started out after her. She knew a sudden impulse to clamp on her skis and start out anyway, but squashed it. That wouldn't help; it'd only make things worse.

The cabin was darkening, as though it were dusk. Sighing, C.J. went to light the lamp. There was nothing to do but wait out the storm and try to keep from going stir-crazy. Deciding that it would be pointless to faint for lack of food, she began rummaging in the cabinets, ignoring the increasing howl of the wind.

She found the bottle of wine again, and debated briefly before setting it on the counter. "That's it, my girl," she murmured to herself, "get drunk on vintage wine. Play cat's cradle if you can find a piece of string. Find a broom and clean the place up. Fix yourself a nice supper. And when you run out of things to do, you can always talk to yourself They say that's the first sign of insanity." She reflected for a moment, then added wryly, "Particularly when you answer yourself."

C.J. fixed herself a tasteless meal of canned chicken and dumplings, drank three glasses of wine, and started to feel sorry for herself. Ruthlessly swallowing the self-pity, she corked the wine again, found a broom, and started to clean the cabin. Energetically.

At the end of half an hour, she had one very clean cabin, a blister on one palm from the rough broom, watering eyes from the dust, and a childish inclination to stick out her tongue at Mother Nature.

Where was the Maestro, damnit? Surely he hadn't started out after her? No. No, he was safe at the lodge. Probably mad and worried, but safe, at least.

Trouble was, she couldn't put much faith in that hope. She knew her Fate, and if he was anything, it was a doer. He was about as likely to sit around and wait for news as she was to take the next shuttle to the moon. And the fact that he was an expert skier did very little to ease her worry. Expert skiers got lost in blizzards.

And if she lost Fate now, because of her thoughtless stupidity in skiing off alone, life wouldn't be worth living.

Standing in front of the blazing fire, C.J. stared into orange flames, her mind very far away. Then a sound caught her attention, and she looked toward the door with a faint, uneasy frown. It was difficult to tell exactly where it had come from, due to the steadily increasing howl of the wind, but something told her that she was no longer totally alone. And she jumped a foot when the door was suddenly flung open with a crash.

He didn't look like a maestro, or an Indian, or a troubadour. He looked like a tired, worried man, the hard anxiety of his face softening with relief as his dark eyes regarded the figure slumped in the aftermath of shock.

He was dressed for warmth and covered with snow, and she heard his rueful voice over the wail of the wind.

"Trust my pixie to go barreling out into an approaching blizzard, and then find the one shelter for miles around. Stay put; I'll let the others know you're all right." Pulling a walkie-talkie from the pocket of his thick jacket, he stepped back outside and closed the door behind him.

Belatedly, C.J. realized that her mouth was hanging open, and hastily shut it.

Ten

When he came back inside the cabin, Fate propped his skis and poles by the door, tossed his knapsack onto the table, and then removed his jacket and hung it neatly on a peg. Silently.

Weak with relief at his safety, C.J. was nonetheless a bit wary. She had a feeling that she was about to experience yet another facet of the man she loved, and this one didn't exactly promise to be comfortable. Any other man would have raged at her for being such an utter fool; this calm silence was a bit unnerving.

Having shed his outer gear and brushed the snow from his person, Fate strolled over to her and placed his hands quite gently on her shoulders. And then he shook her. Hard.

"Don't—you—*ever*," he gritted fiercely, "do that to me again!"

"I *won't* do it again," she managed breathlessly, but Fate wasn't listening. Hard on the heels of the physical shaking came a sensual shaking that was quite wonderful. Emerging from the embrace with her senses spinning, C.J. managed one weak statement. "You shouldn't have come after me—you could have gotten lost."

Fate showed his utter contempt of that by kissing her again.

She finally, reluctantly, pushed him toward one of the chairs. "Sit down. I'll get you some coffee; you look frozen."

Fate pushed a stray lock of hair from his forehead and gave her a mild glare. "I ought to turn you over my knee, you know that, don't you?" he asked wryly, moving to the chair and sitting down.

"How did you find me?" she asked, disregarding that.

"Followed your tracks until about an hour ago. Then I lost them, so I just crossed my fingers and kept going."

"Who did you talk to on the walkie-talkie?" She busied herself making him a cup of coffee.

"A small rescue team combing the slopes for stray skiers, of which you were one. I told them we'd stay here until the storm passes. One of them said this place was always kept stocked with food and wood just in case."

C.J. silently refused to abandon her fanciful story of star-crossed lovers. Before she could say anything, Fate was going on briskly.

"Stop changing the subject, pixie. The point of this little adventure is that you need a keeper! Now, I know that I promised to be patient, but every man has his limits, and today has pushed me well past mine. We're getting married on Valentine's Day—if I can wait that long—and that's all there is to it!"

C.J., her back to him and busy with the coffee, said casually, "I think that's a terrific idea." There was a long silence from behind her.

"C.J.?" His voice was almost inaudible.

Forgetting the coffee, she turned to find him on his feet and looking at her with undisguised hope shining in the purple eyes. Her own voice was very husky when she answered the question there. "Don't you know how much I love you?"

Two long strides brought him to her side. "Pixie . . . are you sure?" he breathed, something about him suggesting that he was holding himself under tight restraint.

She stood on tiptoe to slide her arms around his neck. "Sure? Of course I'm sure. I love you, Fate . . . darling Fate . . . more than anyone else in this world."

For a long moment, he seemed content to drink in the softened, love-drenched expression on her face, the adoring tawny eyes. And then he bent his head, his lips touching hers with shattering tenderness. "Oh, Lord, I love you," he whispered hoarsely. "I thought I'd have to drag you to the altar kicking and screaming."

"Never." She gloried in the feel of his hard body pressed against hers, the closeness of their mingling breath. "I know a good thing when I latch on to one! Every woman should have a slightly crazy Indian brave by her side."

He rested his forehead against hers, a light glowing in his dark eyes which was wonderful to see. "When did you know?"

C.J. smiled wryly. "Unconsciously . . . since that first night. Consciously . . . Remember the party? Everything was happening that day. You'd met the guys for the first time; I'd finally decided that it was time I joined the parade; and then I realized that not only were you wanting some kind of real relationship between us, but I had fallen in love with you without being aware of it."

Fate frowned slightly. "That dance—by the time

the music stopped, you looked as though you'd been kicked in the stomach."

"I was scared to death," she admitted softly, planting a kiss on his chin, the only place she could reach since he'd raised his head. "It happened so fast I didn't know if it was real or insane."

"Why didn't you tell me?"

"That I loved you, or that I was afraid?" she asked.

"Both."

"I didn't tell you how I felt because I *was* afraid— and you knew that I was afraid of something."

"Will you tell me now what you were afraid of?"

C.J. picked her words carefully. "You said once that I only truly came out of myself when I found a challenge; and that was right on target. You challenged me, Maestro—on every level. And I was deathly afraid of losing that." When he would have spoken, she pressed gentle fingers against his lips. "Then—out here alone—I realized that every day with you would bring a new challenge. You're so— damned—unpredictable!" she finished with a laugh.

Fate lifted a hand and caught her fingers, kissing them lightly. "I told you that I did crazy things when I fell in love with a beautiful pixie," he teased gently. "And I promise to be totally unpredictable every day of our lives."

"What more could a woman want. . . ."

Still kissing her fingers, and gazing adoringly into her eyes, he murmured, "I love you, pixie." And then, without altering his tone of voice, added, "The coffee's boiling over."

C.J. blinked at him and then laughed, snatching her hand away and giving him a push toward the table. "Peasant! Go sit down, and I'll make another pot."

Chuckling, Fate walked over to the table while

C.J. hastily removed the boiling pot from the stove and set it on the counter. "There's no need," he told her cheerfully. "I brought a Thermos of coffee with me." He dug into the knapsack.

"You might have told me sooner," she scolded.

"I forgot," he explained disarmingly.

C.J. turned off the stove and went to sit in one of the chairs. "We have to talk," she announced and, reading the gleam in his eyes, added firmly, "about practical things."

Fate cast a longing glance toward the bed. "Do we have to?" he asked mournfully.

"Yes!"

He sighed and poured out a cup of coffee. "Want some of this?" His voice was resigned.

"No, thanks." Pleased to have won a minor point, C.J. was caught off guard when he placed his cup on the table, calmly picked her up, and then sat down with her on his lap.

"Fate!"

"If we *have* to talk, I'm going to make myself comfortable." He started nuzzling her neck.

She leaned determinedly away. "Stop that! Look, if we're going to trip merrily down the aisle, there are a few problems needing to be ironed out first."

"Not if, love—when."

C.J. hastily caught a wandering hand. "*When* we get married, then," she corrected. "But we have to solve the problems first."

"Minor difficulties," he dismissed casually.

"You consider nearly two thousand miles a minor difficulty?"

Fate gave her a mild glare, frustrated because she was now holding both his hands firmly. "I can't think straight when I'm having withdrawal pains," he complained.

"Try," she instructed heartlessly.

"All right, you hard-hearted pixie." He lounged

back in the chair and freed one of his hands to pick up the cup of coffee. Sipping the drink, he added, "Let's hammer it out, point by point."

"First point: you live in Denver, and I live in Boston."

"And you don't want to move so far away from your friends," he finished dryly.

"That's part of it," she admitted, still reluctant to tell him the major reason why it just wouldn't be practical for her to leave Boston. But he was smiling.

"I'm way ahead of you, sweetheart." His voice was casual. "The phone calls this morning finalized a deal I set in motion the day after I met you."

She blinked at him, fascinated. "Really?"

"Uh huh. A friend of mine lives in Boston. He and I graduated law school together, and we've talked from time to time about the possibility of opening our own office. Nothing ever came of it until last week, when I called to find out if he was still interested. He was. Pending your approval, everything's settled."

On the verge of losing her temper at his high-handedness, C.J. was considerably mollified by his last statement. "Taking a lot for granted, weren't you?" she asked tartly.

"Not at all. I meant to follow you to Boston, pixie, whether you liked it or not. And since a man likes to demonstrate his ability to support his future wife, I thought I'd better make sure I had a job in that fair city."

C.J. stirred uneasily and spoke hastily when he placed his cup back on the table with pointed emphasis. "Which brings us to point two. And I don't know if it's going to be a problem—it all depends on how you react to it."

"You terrify me," he said calmly. "What's point two?"

C.J. traced an absent finger along his jaw. "Well . . . do you remember this morning, when I told you I was rich?"

"I remember everything you've ever said to me," he said, his hand—once again free—creeping up underneath her sweater.

She caught his wrist, saying rather desperately, "I wasn't kidding, Maestro!"

His expression altered slowly from lusty interest to comical surprise. "You weren't?"

"I thought you should know," she replied, torn between laughter and uneasiness.

"What kind of salary does a research librarian command? Maybe I should change professions," he said wryly.

"You know better than that." She sighed. "My father and uncle went into business together before I was born. The company grew steadily, and they incorporated, making sure that control remained in their hands. When Daddy died, his shares were left to Siri and me, with the voting stock going to my uncle. And when he died, he left everything to us—mostly to me. Since Siri follows my advice, and since we own the majority of stock, I—more or less—own the company."

"What kind of company?" he asked slowly.

C.J. sighed again. "We make video games, and computers . . . electronic components for aircraft and spacecraft. We're diversified," she ended brightly. "The company's growing by leaps and bounds!"

"I'll bet," he said, obviously thinking of the booming computer industry. And then he started to laugh.

Encouraged by this light-hearted response, C.J. offered hopefully, "I really don't have much to do with the day-to-day running of the company; I just have to worry about major decisions."

"What's the company's name? I may have heard of it."

Sure that he had, C.J. answered hesitantly. "It's called Ben-Car Electronics. For my father and uncle—Ben and Carter."

His eyes widening, Fate whistled softly. "That's one of the best-known electronics firms in the country." His expression was unreadable.

Growing more uneasy, C.J. said, "I promised my uncle that I'd keep it in the family. He—he knew that he was ill a long time before I did, and he set everything up very carefully. I'm not stupid about business, but I don't much like it, and he knew that. He fixed things so that I wouldn't have to get very involved in the company. I have some very good financial advisors, and they take care of things for me."

He stared at her for a long moment, apparently noting her uneasiness, then grinned. "I really lucked out, didn't I?"

Relieved, but still dimly worried that his pride might have taken a battering, she asked, "You don't mind, do you?"

"Mind?" He appeared to chew that one over for a moment. "I'd have to be crazy to mind, wouldn't I?" Then he laughed again. "Tell you what—I'll provide the necessities, and you spring for the luxuries. How's that?"

With a weight off her mind, C.J. leaned closer to him and slipped her arms around his neck. "Sounds like a workable partnership to me," she said.

"Glad you agree." He started to nuzzle her throat. "Anything else to hammer out, or are we agreed on all major points?"

Trying to concentrate, C.J. found it impossible. "I . . . think that about covers it," she murmured huskily. "Anything else is bound to be minor, and we can work it out later."

He lifted his head to give her a look of mock seriousness. "Is that bed comfortable?"

"It sags in the middle," she answered with equal solemnity.

"The better to hold you close, love." He rose to his feet, holding her easily and looking down at her with a glinting smile.

C.J. wasn't about to find fault with his obvious plans for the rest of their day . . . and night. "Better put more wood on the fire," she advised in a helpful spirit.

Fate carried her over to the bed, calmly dropped her into the middle of it, and then headed for the wood stacked in the corner.

"Well, thanks!" she laughed, bouncing once and then sliding inexorably into the quilted depression.

"You're welcome," he responded politely. Having placed three logs on the fire, he came back to the bed and stood beside it, staring down at her. His dark eyes took in her position on the bed—flat on her back with her hands folded over her stomach and an expression of saintly patience on her face as she all but vanished into the bed's sagging middle—and sighed. "What is this, an invitation to ravishment?" he asked courteously.

"Don Juan," she announced, "couldn't ravish somebody in this bed. Fate, this is not going to work; if my weight does this, yours'll make it neatly fold in the middle!"

"Then we'll have to do something about that, won't we?" Briskly, he got to work, bringing logs from the corner to place beneath the sagging springs. Meanwhile, C.J. pulled herself from the quilted valley and unmade the bed, shaking the covers out briskly before remaking it.

"Never know what might have crawled in there," she told Fate darkly as they finished their tasks.

"I know what's about to," he responded, coming toward her.

"You're an insatiable man," she observed severely.

"I certainly am."

C.J. slid her arms around his waist and tilted her head back to look up at him as he drew her close. "Please note that I didn't say I didn't like it," she added.

"That's good, because I'm not about to let you go, pixie," he said unevenly, bending his head, his lips teasing hers apart.

He didn't take advantage of her immediate response, but continued to tease and torment. He kissed one corner of her mouth and then the other, his tongue lightly tracing the sensitive inner skin of her lips. His hands framed her face warmly, preventing her from ending the gentle torture.

She pressed her body against his, moving sensuously with the knowledge he had taught her. Her hands probed beneath his sweater, pulling the tail of his shirt from the waistband of his slacks and finding the firmly muscled flesh beneath it.

Fate groaned softly and abruptly discarded the teasing, taking her mouth in a surge of fiery hunger. His tongue searched and probed and possessed, joining with hers in a blazing encounter.

And then he suddenly put her away from him, informing her in a hoarse voice, "If you don't get out of those clothes right this minute, I'm going to tear them to bits, and you won't have a thing to wear back to the lodge."

"Oh, that would never do." With deliberate slowness, she began to remove her clothes one article at a time, folding each item carefully and placing it on the chair closest to her. By the time Fate had rapidly, carelessly, discarded his own clothing, she was down to panties and bra. He wasted no time in ridding her of the delicate scraps of satin and lace.

"Look what you did," she scolded breathlessly.

Fate dropped the ruined tatters to the floor. "I warned you," he said, immediately sweeping her into his arms and placing her impatiently on the turned-down bed.

C.J. giggled as his weight came down beside her. "Next time I'll pay more attention."

"Or strip faster." He buried his face in her throat, lips moving hotly against soft skin. One leg trapped her restless ones as his hands began to wander hungrily. "Lord, you drive me crazy! Lovely pixie. I love you so much. . . ."

Nearly mindless with desire, C.J. nevertheless distinctly heard two more words whispered against her flesh, and those words caught her full attention. Locking her fingers in his black hair, she pulled his head up, demanding, "What did you say?"

"That I love you," he murmured, kissing her.

But his darkly passionate eyes held a boyishly gleeful expression, and she wasn't deceived. "I love you, too, and what *else* did you say?"

He kissed her again. "Nothing much . . . Clementine Josephine."

Dazedly, she murmured, "He guessed. He finally guessed." Then the full import of his gleeful look sunk in. "No, he didn't guess; he *knew*! Who told you?"

"I've known all along," he told her, nibbling lightly on her lower lip.

C.J. struggled to ignore the distraction. "Fate—I want to know how you found out my name!"

He sighed. "I have other things on my mind right now, Clementine Josephine."

"Tell me!"

Sighing again, Fate propped himself on one elbow and rolled his eyes toward the heavens. "Somebody tell me why I've gotten myself engaged to a shrew," he implored tragically.

"Fate!"

"Probably," he murmured, and then relented at her threatening look. "All right. When I called my soon-to-be partner in Boston last week, I asked him to look up your birth certificate for me. He did, and told me what your name was when I called him back last Wednesday. Satisfied, shrew?"

"Was that legal?" she asked suspiciously.

He looked wounded. "Certainly it was legal."

"I don't believe you."

"Strangely enough, that doesn't surprise me."

"And you've been guessing about my name all along, you deceitful lawyer! Was it fun?"

"Of course. I wouldn't have done it otherwise."

She sighed, then gave him a guarded look. "Well, now you know my shameful secret. If you want to back out of the wedding, I'll understand."

"I think your name's adorable," he said, once more leaning over to explore her throat. "And I wouldn't back out of the wedding if your name was Genghis Khan."

"My word, the man's besotted!" she cried in delight, her arms stealing back around his neck.

"Clearly. He's also on the brink of insanity. I *hope* you're finished talking, pixie . . ."

"Well, if you have something more interesting in mind—" Her teasing words were cut off abruptly as Fate's mouth captured hers, and C.J. gave herself up totally to the blissful wonder of his touch.

As though it were the first time for them, his hands moved over her body softly, lavishing butterfly touches until her senses were spinning wildly. He teased and tormented, his fingers skimming lightly over her lower belly and upper thighs, always just avoiding the heart of her burning desire. His lips caressed her breasts hotly, teeth nipping lightly, tongue swirling avidly.

She moaned and twisted restlessly, her trembling fingers shaping his shoulders, sliding down over the rippling muscles of his back, then snaking around to touch his flat stomach. Knowing, now, what pleased and excited him, she allowed her hands to tease and explore, rewarded by his harsh groan and muttered words.

"You're so sweet . . . Lord, pixie, how did I ever exist without you? I love you so much. . . ."

C.J. gasped when his fingers at last found their target, her breath catching in her throat, and her body arching instinctively. "Fate—! Oh, please, darling . . ."

He rose above her. "Darling . . . you turn that word to magic," he rasped softly, dark eyes glowing down on her. And then his body moved, possessing her, making her his and giving himself to her for all time.

C.J. felt the splintering tension building within her, holding him, moving with him. She wanted desperately to lose herself in him, to become a flesh-and-blood part of him. And for a timeless moment, she felt that it had happened. She fell into his purple eyes, into the heart of a purple star and the Indian she loved.

She cried out his name raggedly, hearing dimly her own name torn from his throat harshly, rapture claiming them both.

"It's indecent," C.J. murmured a long while later as Fate drew the blankets and quilt over their cooling bodies. "The middle of the day! . . ."

"That's the charm of it, love," he replied in a

satisfied tone, arranging her comfortably at his side.

"Are we going to stay here all day?" she asked in a scandalized voice.

"Do you have somewhere else to go?" he asked politely.

"Now that you mention it . . . no."

"Well then?"

"We're being very lazy."

"Not at all. Would you like to know how many calories we just burned?"

"You're terrible."

"Don't be sassy, Clementine Josephine, or I'll paddle that delightful backside."

She sighed. "If you're going to use that horrible name, at least use the shortened version I answered to as a kid."

"Which is?"

"Tina."

"That's sweet." He kissed her forehead. "But I like the long version, too. I'll use it whenever you get too sassy."

"Use it in front of anybody, and I'll divorce you."

"I'll keep that in mind."

"Do that. By the way, there's something I've been meaning to tell you for days. The girls never did believe your parasite and laser beam story."

"What?" He sounded shocked. "You mean I failed?"

" 'Fraid so. Jan hit me with it the night of that damned party. They played along with it because it tickled them." She laughed suddenly. "Now you know why the guys watched you as though they were looking for horns and a tail."

Fate pulled her over on top of him. "Your friends have been absolutely no help to me," he complained wryly. "They wouldn't tell me your name—"

"Which you unscrupulously discovered for yourself."

"—and they never mentioned your company," he finished, ignoring her interruption.

"They told you everything else. The only things left for me to tell you were my name, the company, and that I love you."

He grinned up at her. "That last sounds the best. I'll never grow tired of hearing it."

"Good. I'll never grow tired of saying it. You're a crazy, unpredictable Indian, Maestro, and I love you." C.J. rained kisses over his face, adding seductively, "About that dream I had . . ."

"How you keep harping on that dream!"

"Well, I *have* to know if I was really dreaming."

"I'll never tell."

C.J. sighed despairingly. "And I'll never know!"

"If you're real good . . . I'll tell you on our twentieth anniversary. And not an hour before."

"I'll get it out of you before then," she said confidently. "As a matter of fact . . ."

"As a matter of face what? I don't trust the gleam in your eyes, pixie!"

"I was just thinking about that lewd suggestion I woke you up with one morning."

"Great minds. I was thinking about it, too." He pulled her head down, his tongue lightly tracing her lower lip.

"Want to bet I get the truth out of you?" she whispered.

"Oh, love," he said softly between kisses, "did no one ever tell you never to bet against Fate? . . ."

THE EDITOR'S CORNER

LOVESWEPT'S month of March blows in with A **TRUSTWORTHY REDHEAD** but hardly goes out like a lamb with **TEMPORARY ANGEL.** Each of our four offerings for the month of shamrocks and shillelaghs has been selected to be as haunting as an Irish folksong and as spritely as a jig. We hope you enjoy all of our romances.

Sabrina Courtney, Iris Johansen's heroine in **THE TRUSTWORTHY REDHEAD** #35, may not be Irish, but she's as high-spirited as a colleen and as lovely, too. Remember Honey Winston's promise to Lance's cousin, Alex Ben Rashid, in this month's work by Iris, **THE GOLDEN VALKYRIE?** Well, in her next offering Iris has Honey deliver on that promise by sending Sabrina, **THE TRUSTWORTHY REDHEAD,** to Alex on his birthday. And what a way for Sabrina to deliver Honey's birthday greetings! It will take your breath away just as it takes Alex's away. As fast-paced and emotion-charged as all Iris's books, **THE TRUST-WORTHY REDHEAD** has, too, one of the most moving of her characters. He is a boy named David and I trust he'll touch your heart and linger in your memory.

There should be leprechauns dancing on the pages of Carla Neggers's, **A TOUCH OF MAGIC,** #36. This romances between Brad "Magic" Craig and Sarah Blackstone is so whimsical and amusing that you would think those mischievous elves of Irish folklore had had a hand in complicating the course of their true love!

(continued)

And two more different kinds of people you can't imagine than the Superbowl winning quarterback hero and the blueblood heroine! Typical of Carla's other delightfully offbeat LOVESWEPT romances, **A TOUCH OF MAGIC** will leave you chuckling long after you've closed the book.

The next leaf on our "four leaf clover" of offerings for March is the witty Marie Michael romance **IR-RESISTIBLE FORCES,** #37. Shane McCallister's editor at *Rendezvous Magazine* decides to bring down a peg or two his bright and wise-cracking reporter. And this he attempts to do by sending her to interview the reigning romantic hero of the silver screen. Rather than finding a vacuous pretty boy, Shane discovers in Nick Rutledge a sensitive and intelligent man. But their personal story is a hard one for Shane to cover—especially if she wants it to have a happy ending! Marie Michael learned to speak English and to dream a little by watching old movies on television. She brings all the verve and enthusiasm of beautiful memories of her favorite pastime to this charming romance.

Ah-h, last but never, never least, is Billie Green's **TEMPORARY ANGEL,** #38. This is a love story as fresh and vibrant as a shamrock and as fun-filled as the St. Paddy's Day parade. Angie Jones is Senator Sam Clements's **TEMPORARY ANGEL.** And Angie is quite sure their attraction must remain just that—temporary. How could a United States Senator succeed with the electorate if he had a sharp-tongued woman and controversial writer like Angel as his wife? Well, Sam knows the answer to that one, but he can't persuade Angie. Then he campaigns to convince her and never was there such an exciting attempt to win a positive vote! But this is a heartwarming romance, too, as well as deliciously amusing. We're awfully pleased and proud for Billie who has achieved such a large following with only three published romances to her credit.

No need to beware the Ides of March with LOVE-SWEPTS to keep you company!

Warm wishes that you may have the "Luck of the Irish" next month and always,
Sincerely,

Carolyn Nichols

Carolyn Nichols
   Editor
LOVESWEPT
Bantam Books, Inc.
666 Fifth Avenue
New York, NY 10103

LOVESWEPT

Love Stories you'll never forget by authors you'll always remember

☐	21603	**Heaven's Price** #1 Sandra Brown	$1.95
☐	21604	**Surrender** #2 Helen Mittermeyer	$1.95
☐	21600	**The Joining Stone** #3 Noelle Berry McCue	$1.95
☐	21601	**Silver Miracles** #4 Fayrene Preston	$1.95
☐	21605	**Matching Wits** #5 Carla Neggers	$1.95
☐	21606	**A Love for All Time** #6 Dorothy Garlock	$1.95
☐	21607	**A Tryst With Mr. Lincoln?** #7 Billie Green	$1.95
☐	21602	**Temptation's Sting** #8 Helen Conrad	$1.95
☐	21608	**December 32nd . . . And Always** #9 Marie Michael	$1.95
☐	21609	**Hard Drivin' Man** #10 Nancy Carlson	$1.95
☐	21610	**Beloved Intruder** #11 Noelle Berry McCue	$1.95
☐	21611	**Hunter's Payne** #12 Joan J. Domning	$1.95
☐	21618	**Tiger Lady** #13 Joan Domning	$1.95
☐	21613	**Stormy Vows** #14 Iris Johansen	$1.95
☐	21614	**Brief Delight** #15 Helen Mittermeyer	$1.95
☐	21616	**A Very Reluctant Knight** #16 Billie Green	$1.95
☐	21617	**Tempest at Sea** #17 Iris Johansen	$1.95
☐	21619	**Autumn Flames** #18 Sara Orwig	$1.95
☐	21620	**Pfarr Lake Affair** #19 Joan Domning	$1.95
☐	21621	**Heart on a String** #20 Carla Neggars	$1.95
☐	21622	**The Seduction of Jason** #21 Fayrene Preston	$1.95
☐	21623	**Breakfast In Bed** #22 Sandra Brown	$1.95
☐	21624	**Taking Savannah** #23 Becky Combs	$1.95
☐	21625	**The Reluctant Lark** #24 Iris Johansen	$1.95

Prices and availability subject to change without notice.

Buy them at your local bookstore or use this handy coupon for ordering:

Bantam Books, Inc., Dept. SW, 414 East Golf Road, Des Plaines, Ill. 60016

Please send me the books I have checked above. I am enclosing
$_____ (please add $1.25 to cover postage and handling). Send
check or money order—no cash or C.O.D.'s please.

Mr/Ms_____

Address_____

City/State_____ Zip_____

SW—3/84

Please allow four to six weeks for delivery. This offer expires 9/84.